Cabana Corpse

A Cassie Hall Mystery

by

Sherry Lodge

Copyright 2017 by Sherry Lodge

For information, email **Cozy Cat Press**, cozycatpress@aol.com or visit our website at: www.cozycatpress.com

COZY CAT PRESS

ISBN: 978-1-946063-22-9

Printed in the United States of America

Cover design by Paula Ellenberger
www.paulaellenberger.com

1 2 3 4 5 6 7 8 9 10

Dedicated to Winston

Chapter 1

An enormous red and white striped cabana rested against the cloakroom door, waiting to be assembled. The Parkstone cats—Jet-Setter and Cashmere—crowded around the concierge desk to investigate some packages that had just arrived from our New York headquarters. *These must be the swim caps*, I thought, as I unwrapped the fancy paper and opened the large box. As soon as it opened, Jet-Setter scrambled inside and curled up on the teal swim caps. The perfect way for residents to kick off summer!

As I lifted Jet-Setter out of the box, I noticed the swim caps were monogrammed with the letter 'P'. My boss Royce Baxter had thought of everything. Cashmere meeeowed and dipped her paws into the box. *Now, if I could just keep the fur balls away long enough so I could hand the swim caps out to residents and check their names off my list in an orderly fashion....* In two days, the pool would open—just in time for Memorial Day Weekend. I knew Parkstonians would want their swim caps before opening day and the inaugural swim club meeting.

And for after their swim there were matching teal monogrammed towels. I'd thought the swim caps were enough of a good sentiment, but now seeing the fluffy, monogrammed towels under the matching swim caps, I thought that extra effort would go a long way with residents.

Then I noticed a silver box that Cashmere was nudging across the desk with her nose. I snatched it from her and opened it. It was a dainty box of chocolate truffles: white chocolate, dark chocolate, some topped with pistachios, others with ornate zig zag designs and raspberries. What was even better than a dip in the pool? A dip into the truffle box.

I pulled out a dark chocolate and raspberry truffle, and was about to take a bite when Mr. Gillrot walked up to the concierge desk, wearing his typical plaid button-down shirt, khaki pants and leather sandals. He took one look at the swim caps and scoffed, "That's the only problem with winter; it's followed by summer."

I picked up a teal stretchy hat and said with a smile, "Swim cap?"

"No," he said. "It's either too hot to be in the scorching pool or I'm too lazy. Either way, I won't need a swim cap." He looked at the rest of the box's contents. "Or a towel. And I see there's a cabana again. That might be the only part of the pool I like."

"There's always the indoor pool," I said, swinging the cap in his direction.

"There's no way out with you, Cassie, is there?" he said. "You always have a comeback."

"And now *you* have a swim cap," I said, checking Mr. Gillrot's name off the list.

"Well, all right, Cassie," he said. "But if I get a sunburn on that rooftop pool, you're going to be the first to hear about it."

I nodded and grimaced, and hoped that for both our sakes he'd wear sunscreen. Mr. Gillrot left and I was about to indulge in the chocolate raspberry truffle when my eye caught the enormous bright red and white striped pool cabana that headquarters had sent for me—their trusty concierge—to construct poolside on the Parkstone's rooftop. Each summer they'd send a new cabana I had to wrestle with in order to provide the residents a lounging area for respite from the sun. This year was no different. I placed the *"Will be back shortly,"* sign on my desk, hiked the cabana onto a dollie, and took the elevators up to the rooftop.

The humidity on the rooftop made my shirt stick to my back, as I tried to balance the poles of the cabana. Jet-Setter and Cashmere, the Parkstone cats watched my efforts from a chaise across from the pool. "Meeeoww," one roared as a slight breeze tipped the cabana over. I hugged it as it leaned right and managed to move the poles back to center. Then I made sure the stakes were deep enough into the ground, so that the cabana wouldn't tip over.

This light breeze was great for cooling off, but it made the cabana assembly more unwieldy. Once I got all four stakes in the grass and the fabric panels stretched onto the poles, I gathered the cats and headed back to the lobby. Phew!

I approached the concierge desk and took away the *"Will be back shortly sign,"* when the phone rang.

I answered with my most official voice: "Thank you for calling the Parkstone; this is concierge Cassie Hall speaking. How may I help you?"

On the other end I could hear someone crying and then a shaky voice, "Cassie? I have horrible news for you. There's been a flood!"

I didn't recognize the voice. "With whom am I speaking?"

"It's Mrs. Olive, Cassie—the swim club leader. There's a flood."

"In your apartment?" I said.

"Yes, Apartment 704," she said. "I'm here, but I don't have enough buckets for all the water that's coming from the apartment above me."

"I'll be right there," I said, hanging up the phone and picking up a swim cap. If there *was* a flood, the cap could come in handy. I crossed Mrs. Olive's name off the list.

*****

I took the elevator to Apartment 704 and knocked loudly several times. On the third try, a frantic Mrs. Olive opened the door.

"Cassie! I'm so glad you're here. Look what I've had to contend with," she said, pointing to a row of Teflon pots filled to the brim with water along the wall. She was wearing a rain jacket, rain boots, and I handed her the swim cap. "To save your hair," I said. "Courtesy of the Parkstone."

"Why, thank you, Cassie," she said. "You always think of everything." She put on the swim cap. "Five years I've lived in this apartment, and no problems. Now *this!*" She pointed into the bathroom and I followed.

A gush of water flowed from the ceiling. What a disaster. "You can't stay here," I said. "I'll call maintenance right away, and get you set up in a guest room."

Mrs. Olive, who had put the swim cap on, nodded. "I'd like that very much."

"Gather what you'd like to take," I said, ushering her out of the bathroom and away from the flood. She went to her bedroom to get her belongings. And I placed a quick call to maintenance who said they were on their way. As I was talking on the phone, I stood in her living room and noticed a large collection of DVDs lined up along the wall next to her TV. One caught my eye: *Rocky Lakes*, a drama set in Colorado. How strange? I'd only heard of the movie because I used to live in Colorado, but when it was produced I'd been too young to watch it.

Then I turned around. I shouldn't have been spying on residents. I was here to make their life at the

Parkstone better. "Mrs. Olive, maintenance will be here shortly," I said. "But we should leave before the entire place floods."

She appeared in the doorway, holding a full suitcase and still wearing the swim cap. "I'm ready."

I nodded. "Let's get you to the guest room."

She looked over at the DVDs, then said, "I hope the water doesn't do too much damage."

"It won't," I assured her, "but we should probably go now."

We left with the sound of rushing water, and I hoped maintenance would be there soon. I got Mrs. Olive settled in the twelfth-floor guest room. It had a kitchen and bedroom and a balcony that overlooked the courtyard.

And the furniture was grand. There was an amazing traditional antique white armoire, that I knew my mom would love. She was a nurse with a keen eye for furniture and interior design, and she was coming to visit me at the Parkstone in just a couple of days.

"How long do you think it will take maintenance to fix the leak?" she said.

"It depends," I said, "but at least for now you have a place to stay. And the pool will be open in only two days."

"Okay, Cassie," she said, letting go of her luggage bag. "The sooner I can get back to my apartment, the better."

I left Mrs. Olive to settle into the guest room and headed back to the lobby where I saw Mr. Rhodes and his Chihuahua Moola standing at the concierge desk. Then I saw him dip into the box on the desk and pull out two swim caps.

"Wait!" I said as I approached the desk, "I need to check your name off the list so I know you got a swim cap."

"Consider it done. I've got one for myself and Mrs. Rhodes," he said, "although, I'd like one for Moola, too. Any Chihuahua-sized caps?"

"Not at this moment," I said, knowing that that wouldn't be possible. "The Parkstone swim caps are one size fits all."

"For next year, it would be great to have one for Moola," he said, with a plastered smile on his face.

"Right," I said. "I'll mention it to Royce and see what we can do."

"And that's why we love living here."

"Truffle?" I said.

He smiled. "Another reason this place is great."

For every leak at the Parkstone, there was a truffle to make up for it. Then the thought crossed my mind. Mrs. Olive might want a truffle too. I place the *"Will be back shortly,"* sign on the concierge desk and headed to the twelfth floor with the box of truffles.

I knocked on the guest room door. No answer. I knocked again. Still no answer. I knocked a third time even louder and then from behind the door, Mrs. Olive said nervously, "Who is it?"

"It's me, Cassie," I said. "With truffles."

"I don't believe you."

I gulped. That was unexpected. "It really is me— Cassie." I held the box of truffles up to the peephole.

"I don't want truffles," she said. I gulped again. What I thought was going to be a nice gesture seemed to rattle her.

Then there was a long pause. "On second thought, maybe *one* truffle will be okay."

She opened the door slightly. I pinched a raspberry truffle and placed it on her open hand. "Call down to the concierge desk if you need anything," I said.

"You got it, Cassie," she said, and shut the door.

I walked swiftly to the elevators. *Two more days until the pool was open,* I kept telling myself. That always lifted people's spirits.

I took the elevator to the lobby floor. I finally had a moment of downtime and was just about to eat that raspberry truffle when the phone rang. It was my boss, Royce Baxter, owner of the Parkstone and Baxter Enterprises. His call was unexpected and I was thankful I'd answered the phone in my official Parkstone greeting.

It sounded like he was walking down a busy New York street. "I had a minute and wanted to check in with everything at the Parkstone," he said. "I know things have been on edge after Mrs. Thornwhistle's murder."

I grimaced. *On edge or over the edge?* "Since the murder, every resident has been worried that it's going to happen again. I think many of them would take killer rents over killer residents."

"Clever, Cassie," he said. "Did you get the cabana, swim caps and towels? And the truffles? I know the building's swim club will start again this season. Make some time to spend at the pool."

What Royce didn't know was that I was planning a vacation with my fiancé Eric to the eastern shore for a week this summer. Planning a vacation was so much easier than planning a wedding. We'd already rented the house, scoped out good seafood restaurants, and I already had my bikini and flip flops picked out: sea foam green and purple Kate Spade polka dots. "The swim caps look sharp, and the truffles look delicious."

"Well, have one, Cassie, and make sure the residents enjoy them, too."

"I haven't had time," I said, eyeing the decadent chocolate and raspberry truffle on the side of the concierge desk. "I've been busy all morning. There's a leak in Mrs. Olive's apartment, and the pool cleaners mixed up the days they were supposed to come, so they showed up today instead of tomorrow. There was an ambulance called for resident Penelope Rhodes, who fainted in her apartment. Apartment 202 is being re-painted and their neighbor Mrs. Canterbury has been complaining of nausea because of the fumes. Mr. Gillrot got locked out on his eleventh-floor balcony for two hours in the heat."

"How did he get down?" Royce asked.

"He flagged down another resident, Ben Harrison, who was in the observatory looking up at him with the telescope." Life at the Parkstone could be crazy.

"I had no idea, Cassie," he said. "That's a lot of events and it isn't even noon."

I ate the truffle. It was now or never.

"Before, I go," he said, "what's the good news?"

"The truffles are delicious, and…" I said, trying to think of a follow up, "there hasn't been a murder in three months." I knocked on the concierge desk for good luck.

I said goodbye to Royce, thinking my next big task was waiting. Then I heard someone behind me at the desk clear their throat. I turned around and there stood Mr. and Mrs. Berry, who were at the Parkstone today to meet with our leasing agent Lillian and sign a lease. Jet-setter and Cashmere scampered on top of the concierge desk to greet the new residents.

"A murder?" Mrs. Berry said. I guessed she'd overheard my phone conversation.

I nodded. In fact, there had been three.

She continued, "Here? That seems absurd."

"It's true," I said.

She looked up at her husband. "Well, dear, what do you think?"

He looked at me. "We're empty nesters," he said. "We just need a quiet place to settle that's walkable." He looked at the swim caps.

"It's swimmable, too," I said. "The pool opens Thursday."

"Dear," he said, looking at his wife. "I think we need to give it a try."

"Luxury suits everybody," I said, smiling.

"Even murderers," Mrs. Berry said under her breath.

Lillian appeared moments later with a huge smile. The Berrys said their goodbyes and soon after they left, Mr. Harold Eager walked up to the desk and said, "There you are."

I smiled. "How are you, Mr. Eager?"

"Well, I'm all right, Cassie. Just stopped by to say hi."

"Truffle?"

"Don't mind if I do," he said. I smiled and said, "Swim cap?"

"Oh no," he said, waving a hand. "I don't swim. I'm terrified of the water."

"You'll get over that once you see the rooftop pool," I said. The pool was gorgeous. There was the large cabana to the right, and plum trees that grew near the rooftop entrance. The pool was Olympic-sized with a diving board, and a clubhouse behind it. The clubhouse was a good place for residents to seek shade and relax and enjoy snacks and refreshments. There were chaises poolside and large chestnut trees that lined the back lawn of the pool area where there was a grill for barbequing. But I guess some, like Mr. Eager, weren't interested in swimming.

"No," he said, "I'm pretty sure I won't. I've been afraid of the water ever since I was a kid. I'm 70 years old. I'm not going to start liking it now."

"Suit yourself," I said. "But take a cap just in case."

He smiled and accepted the Parkstone swim cap. I checked his name off the list. And then I got an idea. "You could always join the swim club. Their first practice is this Saturday. That might help you get over your fear."

"Well, now, I've got the right gear in case I decide to," he said with a smile.

In two days, everything at the Parkstone would be a dive in the pool!

Chapter 2

Thursday got there soon enough. It was my day off and I decided to join the Swim Club for a quick swim in the morning before attending to my other tasks, such as choosing my wedding cake designer and narrowing down my wedding guest list. The pool was a great perk of living and working at the Parkstone. I walked past the red and white striped cabana which I'd spent hours putting together a day earlier. The sides were sturdy and the poles were securely fastened in the ground, so I hoped it wouldn't blow away in the wind.

I spread my towel alongside the chaise next to the cabana, and wondered if maybe the cabana's shaded polyester panels would provide better protection from the wind. I soaked in some more rays. On second thought, the heat felt great on my skin, and I was happy to be sporting my new Ralph Lauren red and purple plaid halter bikini.

It was nice to get away from the concierge desk for a day. And it would be good to mingle with the residents at a time when I wasn't behind the desk.

"Hello!" I heard a shrill voice call from the shade of the clubhouse. It was Dot Olive. She stepped out onto the pool deck wearing a ruffled skirt bathing suit in a green and yellow palm tree print. She'd wrapped her towel around her waist, as if she'd already been in the pool.

"Is somebody here for swim club?" she said.

I nodded. When I was younger and living in Cherry Creek, Colorado, I would go swimming in the lakes and neighborhood pool all the time. But that was years ago. And while I could still swim, my strokes probably weren't as good as they were back then. Dot Olive walked over to the chestnut tree in the poolside clearing next to the clubhouse, and slung her towel over one of the lower branches—straightening it out so it would dry. It was a scorcher, so I didn't think it would take very long.

Soon after, the rest of the group began to show up. There was Mrs. Penelope Rhodes in a magenta pink bikini, and her husband, Dash Rhodes, and their dog Moola, who sported a small red and white striped inner tube. There was Harold Eager, who was trying to get over his fear of water, and was wearing a Parkstone inner tube as he parked himself on the edge of a chaise. Then there was Mary Chris Farley, with wisps of her fishtail braid emerging out of her swim cap. She was standing next to Mrs. Lydia Kemper, who complained about the swim cap and the floating devices and who was wearing her jean shorts and an embroidered t-shirt. And then a surprise participant—the new resident, Mrs. Berry, showed up wearing a large straw hat, sunglasses and holding what looked to be a refreshing glass of sparkling water with a lemon twist.

I was surprised to see her. "Isn't this your move-in day?" I said, as she took a seat on the edge of the pool.

"And what a glorious day it is!" she said, tipping her hat up and looking into the sky. "Mr. Berry is helping the movers; we plan to move in in a day, and I thought it was the perfect opportunity to skip out for a break," she said. "I wanted to meet some of the other residents."

Her red lipstick looked stunning. Mrs. Olive looked somewhat intimidated or maybe jealous—it was difficult to tell which, the way her face was scrunched up, as she glared at Mrs. Evelyn Berry, who was dipping her red-manicured feet in the pool. "Dare I say we go in?"

Then Mrs. Olive scoffed. And before I knew it, the two of them were in the pool facing each other. At the same time, Mrs. Berry and Mrs. Olive both said, "It's you!" Then they glared at each other, and Mrs. Olive said, "Guess you never know who lives at the Parkstone."

Mrs. Berry held her chin high and said, "Guess not." Then suddenly, they both seemed to be just fine. *What was that all about?*

Mrs. Olive clapped her hands. "For the last three years, I've been the leader of the swim club," she said. "So, I know a bit about swimming. First things first. Everyone apply suntan lotion. Then let's work on our stretches." She did a quick stretches demo, but no one seemed too enthralled. "And stay hydrated…" Mrs. Berry held her glass up in a toast. Mrs. Olive continued. "I know there are some beginners here today," she said, glancing over at Mr. Eager, "so for those of you who are experienced, go ahead. And those of you who may need lessons—well—Dot Olive is here!" She pointed to herself with a triumphant look on her face.

Mrs. Olive seemed very comfortable talking in front of a group of people. Her movements were almost theatrical. Unfortunately, nobody seemed interested in lessons. Mr. Eager wrestled with the inner tube, trying to get out of it. "I think I'm going to pass today," he said. "The only step I got to was the sunscreen part. I really don't think I'm cut out for this."

"The best way to get over a fear is to just jump in," Mrs. Olive said, shaking a finger at Mr. Eager. "Like this," she said, as she dove and splashed into the pool. "Come on in!"

Mr. Eager backed away. "I don't think so," he said. "Not today. I'll come back tomorrow when I'm a little more courageous—or nuts. One or the other."

Mrs. Berry gently kicked water onto the ledge at the side of the pool. "At least stay awhile," she said. "One could get a lovely tan up here on the rooftop."

He shuddered. "Yes, and I'm not too keen on the sun either," he said. "Maybe this was the wrong club for me."

I gasped. We didn't want to lose a member of the swim club. There were already so few members.

Mrs. Olive who was hanging off the side of the pool said, "Come back tomorrow?"

"I'll be here," Mr. Eager said, gathering his towel and sandals and heading out the rooftop door.

Minus one already. I wasn't surprised. The swimming club was the most difficult one to promote. It was the least attended group at the Parkstone along with bocce ball and fly fishing.

"Cassie," Mrs. Olive said, holding onto the side of the pool, and splashing water with her feet. "Jump in!"

I crept into the water through the shallow end. I was hoping the lifeguard was on duty, but she was only there on certain days of the week. Mrs. Berry followed by saying, "You don't have to twist my arm. It's hot as an oven today," and she walked gracefully into the pool. Mary Chris took a phone call then said she'd see us later. She was such a recluse. Mrs. Kemper finally made it into the pool, but only after Mrs. Olive promised her a dozen blueberry cupcakes.

As we watched Mrs. Olive show off her aquatic skills. Penelope asked where Mrs. Olive had learned to swim. Mrs. Olive had perfected her backstroke and breaststroke, and her butterfly was quicker than anyone's at the Parkstone.

"I took lessons when I was younger," she said. "I lived out in California. If you're going to go to the beach, well, you better learn how to swim. And maybe boogie board. And surf."

I sensed there was a lot about Mrs. Olive I didn't know. I had thought she was from the Midwest. Her accent was definitely Midwestern. Then she looked flustered. "Well, enough about me. Let's swim!"

With that, we all decided to swim. Even Moola, the Rhodes' dog, got her feet wet.

*****

Saturday mornings were always the best. They were usually quiet, and there were enough tasks to keep me busy. This one was especially great, because it was already a couple days after the pool had opened, and everything had gone swimmingly.

The first thing I had to do was building rounds. I placed the *"Will be back shortly,"* sign on the counter. I checked the time—it was 10 a.m. The swim club would be meeting. I checked the courtyard first and the grounds looked fine—nothing unusual. *Yes, Saturdays were great.* Then I took the elevator upstairs, with Jet-setter and Cashmere, the Parkstone cats, in tow.

The pool looked serene, and the deck was vacant as I stepped out onto the rooftop. The tunes from the song *Copacabana* were playing on the radio in the club house. Then Jet-setter darted past me, nearly knocking me over, as I almost fell into a nearby plum tree. *That furball!* I steadied myself with a plum tree branch. "What's gotten into you?" I said, as the fur ball charged ahead. I picked up Cashmere and raced to catch up with Jet-Setter, who had made it halfway down the steps before abruptly stopping and backing away.

Suddenly, chills ran up my arms. "Jet-Setter?" I said. I turned to follow his stare across the pool area into the poolside clearing, the grassy area next to the clubhouse.

The cabana that was usually open and intact near the poolside chaises had collapsed onto the grass—a big heap of red and white striped fabric.

I couldn't believe it had collapsed after I'd spent so much time putting it together!

Then I saw legs, glistening in the sunlight, sticking out from under it. I gasped. I was standing so close I could lift up one of the cabana's panels. I did, and under the red and white fabric, there was a body wearing a signature palm tree print bikini and a teal Parkstone swim cap. I knew exactly who it was. It was Mrs. Olive. She was lying face down on the grass under the cabana!

"Mrs. Olive?" I said. But she was unresponsive. I grabbed the pool cleaner net with the long pole that was next to the club house and managed to turn her over. Her face didn't look good. Cashmere and Jet-Setter stayed near the chairs. I felt for a pulse, but Mrs. Olive didn't have one.

And that's when I suspected that Mrs. Olive had been murdered in cold blood.

No one else was around. What about the swim club? I checked the club house, but no one was there. I switched off the music. Wasn't the swim club meeting supposed to have started by this time? Where was everyone? And why was Mrs. Olive dead?

I reached for my cellphone in my dress pocket to call 911. They promised to send detectives over right away. I was surprised they didn't ask, "The Parkstone, *again?*" I wanted to investigate the crime scene before they got here. My fiancé, homicide detective Eric Peters, would be on the scene shortly, and if I wanted information about the case, I'd need to start sleuthing before he arrived. I took one last look at the corpse and shuddered: *And I thought today was going to be as easy as a lap in the pool.*

I walked over to the chaises along the side of the pool. There was a monogrammed 'P' for Parkstone towel on one of the chaises. That indicated that someone else had been at the pool with Mrs. Olive. The towel was dry, which meant the swimmer may not have gone in the water. What swimmer wouldn't swim? *Mr. Eager. He was deathly afraid of the water.* I had one suspect.

I stepped off of the rooftop and back inside the building. I had to get my wits about me. I was standing in the vestibule when I heard someone rounding the corner. The footsteps got louder, and I heard the chiming of a bracelet or maybe it was a key ring? I held my breath. Could this be the killer coming back to the crime scene?

Then the footsteps stopped. Mr. Rhodes peered his face around the corner. "What's got you so shaken?" he said. His Chihuahua Moola's dog collar chimed as she paraded around the corner. Then, I was shocked when she shook her wet fur on my legs and my A-line hot pink lace Laundry dress. *Gross.*

"I'm fine," I said. "But there's a situation at the pool. I'll have to ask you to stay away until the detectives arrive." I thought about the towel on the chaise. *Everything is evidence.* Even Mr. Rhodes showing up right now at the crime scene was suspicious.

"Moola and I are here for the swim club, Cassie," he said. "Are you telling me we can't attend?"

I looked him squarely in the eye. "Swim club's cancelled."

"Why?" he said. "I hope there's a good reason for it." He paused. "I was getting good at the backstroke."

"There's been a murder," I said. "And the rooftop is off limits to Parkstone residents until the detectives get this all straightened out."

"Can do," said Mr. Rhodes. He picked up Moola. "There's always the fly fishing club."

As he left, I went back onto the rooftop. I noticed, not far from Mrs. Olive's body, there was a towel hanging on one of the chestnut tree branches. *That must be Mrs. Olive's towel.*

In the clubhouse, there was a champagne flute half full of sparkling water. The one Mrs. Berry had yesterday. Did she leave it here? Or was this a clue that she was at the pool already this morning? Outside of the clubhouse, the umbrella at the pool table wasn't even opened. There was a sheet of paper with inspirational swimming quotes written down, most likely by Mrs. Olive. It was secured to the table with a large rock. Was that what someone had used to hit her over the head? Who else had been here with Mrs. Dot Olive?

Just then, the detectives rushed through the rooftop doors. My fiancé, Detective Eric Peters, came up to me first. "Are you all right?" he asked.

"I'm fine, but Mrs. Olive is dead," I said, trying to keep myself from crying. I was on the job and I needed to stay composed.

"When did you find her?"

"No more than fifteen minutes ago," I said.

He surveyed the pool area, "Anything else suspicious?"

I took a second to think about it. "Not that I know of, except this is the time the swim club is supposed to meet and no one's here."

"You found her alone, face up under the cabana?"

Not exactly. "No," I said. "She was face down halfway on the grass and the cement under the cabana. I moved her."

"With what?" he said.

"The pool net," I said, embarrassed now that I'd been trying to decipher clues in the case.

"Well, hopefully that's the extent of your sleuthing," he said with a sideways glance. "Anything else about Mrs. Olive herself?"

"She really was a sweet person. Such a good resident. And she'd had a difficult week. There was a leak in her apartment, and I sensed a rift between her and Mrs. Penelope Rhodes during swim club a couple of days ago. And a suspicious, surprised reaction to Mrs. Berry."

Eric scribbled notes in his notebook. "Good work, Cassie. If you think of any other pertinent details, let me know. The guys and I will decipher her injuries, most likely a blow to the head that caused her to fall on the cement. I'm guessing a fall that caused her to grab onto the cabana and take it down with her. But we'll investigate. And I'll let you know if we have any more questions."

"It might be helpful for me to be around the crime scene to see if there are any clues you might miss."

He eyed me intensely. "Cassie," he said, "please don't sleuth this case. You're brilliant, but whoever did this to Mrs. Olive could strike again if they felt threatened. And I don't want you to be the target."

I nodded. "I'll alert residents to the matter," I said. "And I'll let Royce know. He isn't going to be happy there's been another murder at the Parkstone."

"That all sounds good," he said. "Whatever you do, don't sleuth."

"I wasn't planning on it," I said, already thinking of possible resident motives. "Given my to-do list, I wouldn't possibly have time for sleuthing anyway." This was a lie. I had an extensive to-do list once I got back to the concierge desk. I needed to order last-minute surprise flowers for Mr. Berry's wife, somehow buy sold-out theater tickets for Mr. Gillrot, and submit the maintenance requests for Mrs. Canterbury. But who was I kidding? There was always time for sleuthing.

On my way back inside the building, I ran into Mary Chris wearing a swim suit with geometric shapes and bright neon colors and a towel slung over her shoulder. She'd just walked out onto the rooftop and into the scene of detectives. "What's going on?" she stammered.

"There's been a murder," I said.

Mary Chris looked upset. "Who?" she said in a lowered voice.

The nicest resident at the Parkstone: "Mrs. Dot Olive," I said, cringing.

Mary Chris gasped! She gripped her goggles which she'd almost dropped in surprise. "I must go," she said. "This is horrible. I must leave now."

Her reaction seemed somewhat suspicious, and I wasn't going to let a potential eyewitness go. "Were you here for the swim club?" I said.

"I was running late. I was just a member, not even a great swimmer at that. Dot was the leader, and truly gave it her all," she said. "She loved the swim club so much. Who would do this?"

I looked at her squarely and said, "The detectives are going to find out."

She nodded and left swiftly, taking the stairs. I took the elevator to the lobby level where Mr. Berry was making a coffee at the coffee station. I reminded myself to place the flower order for Mrs. Berry.

First, I typed a quick letter to my boss, Royce Baxter, informing him of the murder:

Dear Royce,
    It's with a saddened heart I report that a resident's poolside plans took a dark turn today.

This morning I found Mrs. Dot Olive's corpse on the rooftop under the collapsed red and white striped cabana. Detectives are on the scene now, and we should know more shortly. For how long should I close the pool to residents? I believe any such disruption will upset the pool-goers who fancied a summer in the sun.

    Cassie Hall

I sent the fax to Royce Baxter in the New York headquarters and was admiring the large bouquet of flowers sent each week from corporate. This week it was a blooming bouquet of Stargazer lilies and white daisies. Mr. Berry brought his coffee over to the concierge desk. "This place is quite grand," he said. "You're right. I can get used to luxury."

I smiled. Everything at the Parkstone was so peaceful and luxurious, except for the murders.

He continued, "And by any chance, were you able to get the flowers I requested? I need them for tonight. Turns out, with our move to the Parkstone, I forgot it was Mrs. Berry's and my anniversary."

I gasped. He'd just mentioned the flowers to me this morning. With everything else going on, I just didn't have time to place the order. I had to think quickly. The Stargazer lilies were lovely. I pushed the bouquet of flowers toward him on the concierge desk and said. "Yes, these arrived for you this morning."

"My gosh, you really pulled it off!" he said. "Thanks, Cassie, I wasn't sure if it was too last minute. Now I don't have to confess to Evelyn I forgot our anniversary." He smiled and wrapped his arms around the white and purple glass vase. "I should bring these up to our apartment and surprise her with these tonight."

I was glad to see he was settling in and enjoying the amenities. He continued, "Mrs. Berry is at the swim club. She joined the first day we moved in and said she's enjoying it."

I nodded, distracted and.... Wait a minute! Mrs. Berry *wasn't* at the swim club. No one was at swim club. I hadn't see anyone on the rooftop. That was odd. "Mr. Berry," I said, "I'm sorry to inform you that there's been a murder. I'm going to announce it over the speaker system momentarily. But I thought you should know first, so I don't startle you." *Especially since he was carrying a glass vase*, I thought.

"Oh no! I'm rattled. Shaking like a dog in the cold," he said. "Where's Evelyn? Where did it happen?"

"Why don't you put the vase down?" I said, worried that if he didn't, I'd be picking up a sopping mess of Stargazer lilies and white daises from the lobby floor.

"The rooftop swimming pool," I said. "Residents are restricted from the rooftop."

"But Evelyn," he said.

I had to break it to him. "She wasn't at swim club," I said. He shrugged, almost spilling the bouquet assortment. "But then where was she?"

"We'll find out," I said. "Hold tight."

I got the BOSE speaker system and turned it on. "Dear Parkstone residents, I have some grave news to report about fellow resident Dot Olive, who was found dead poolside under the rooftop cabana this morning. Please stay away from the rooftop until the rooftop has been cleared by authorities. I will update each and every one of you once I have more information. Thanks for your understanding in this matter."

Mr. Berry stared at me like he'd seen a ghost. "There's a murderer loose in the Parkstone? I must find Evelyn!" He placed the wobbly vase back on the concierge desk and took his cellphone out of his pocket.

His coffee mug was resting on a nearby side table. He dialed his wife's number three times but no answer. "Evelyn always answers my calls."

My mind began to wonder. *Could there be two murders?* I shuddered. "I'll help you find her," I said. I made an overhead announcement for Evelyn Berry to report to the concierge desk. But after twenty minutes of waiting there was no Mrs. Berry. It looked like while the detectives were solving the Dot Olive mystery, Mr. Berry and I had one of our own.

"I'm sure this is a misunderstanding," I said. "Evelyn will call you back soon."

He looked dismayed. "We must do something."

Then I had an idea. "Let's split up and search for her. I'll start at the rooftop and search all the floors until the seventh and you start here at the lobby and search the floors to the sixth. And we'll find her."

"You got it," he said. "And I'll take the flowers with me, so when I find her I can say 'Happy Anniversary!'"

I headed up to the rooftop and once I was there, I headed straight for the locker rooms. Nothing looked suspicious or out of the ordinary. All of the lockers were shut and locked except for Mrs. Penelope Rhodes' locker, which had a door that was flung open. That was odd. Then I thought about where to find Mrs. Berry. Where would I go if I were a missing resident? The sauna! That was one of the Parkstone's best amenities. I hurried to the sauna, which was right down the hall from the lockers and only a few quick steps away. The orange glow of the sauna lit up the hallway. I peered through the glass. There was Mrs. Berry! She was clad in a black one-piece swimsuit and her sunglasses; a perfect indoors choice.

She waved a manicured hand in my direction. "Cassie!" she said, as I stepped into the sauna. "What brings you all the way up to the rooftop?"

It always confused people to see me wearing my "Cassie Hall, concierge" badge and away from the concierge desk. I was relieved to see her. "Mr. Berry was worried about you," I said, feeling hot in the sauna in my lace Laundry dress. "He said you weren't answering your phone, and, well, there's been a murder, so we're all on edge."

She placed her hands on her cheeks in disbelief. "A murder?" she said. "Who was murdered? Where and why?"

"We don't have all of that information yet," I said. "But it was Mrs. Olive, who I found dead near the pool this morning."

She gasped. "Why I was just there," she said. "In fact, that's where I left my phone. That's why I haven't gotten any of Mr. Berry's calls."

"I'll go with you to get it," I said. "The pool is swarming with detectives."

"That would be great," she said.

We walked out onto the rooftop, and Mrs. Berry made her way through the crowd of detectives. I went up to Eric who look stressed. He had a hand on his forehead and he looked deep in thought.

"How's the investigation?"

He jumped. "Cassie, you scared me," he said. "What are you doing here?"

"I accompanied Mrs. Berry," I said, "She left her cellphone…"

"Right here," Eric said, producing a plastic bag with a cellphone. "Found it on the pool bench. It's evidence. Mrs. Berry will have to wait a few days before she can get this back."

I squirmed. That's not going to go over well. Just then I heard Mrs. Berry scream. She walked right up to Eric and me.

"Cassie, do you hear what they're trying to do?" she said. "My cellphone is my lifeline. And they're trying to take it. There's my mother and Mr. Berry and the kids. And this is just all so crazy."

"And *this* is evidence," Eric said, holding up the bag.

"But, Cassie, do something. They can't do that!" she said.

"Mrs. Berry, you must cooperate with the detectives," I said. "You'll only be without a phone for a couple of days."

Eric nodded. "Sorry, ma'am. Procedure."

"Cassie, dear," she said, as we walked along the pool. "I'm a new tenant, and I can assure you this whole murder investigation debacle has not gone over well with me. I'd greatly appreciate your speaking with Royce and letting him know that I'm one tenant who's a ton upset."

Tenants always wanted a break on rent. And when something went wrong, they always had more bargaining power. I nodded. "I'll let him know." Even though I knew Royce was a stickler for the rules. Him giving Mrs. Berry a break on rent would be a bigger stretch than the Parkstone yoga class. Royce didn't bend the rules.

"*And*," she said, holding her head up high. "Don't bother calling me about it. I won't have a phone to answer. Find me, in person. Good chance I'll be in the sauna. Or the Jacuzzi. Or at home with Mr. Berry."

"Of course," I said, as we walked through the doors into the building. "I'm very sorry for the inconvenience."

"Oh, dear," she said, shaking her head. "Don't call it that. It's much more sinister."

With that, she took her sunglasses from on top of her head and covered her eyes. She pressed the elevator button.

Just then, the rooftop door opened.

It was Eric. "Not so fast, Mrs. Berry," he said. "We'll need you for questioning."

She rolled her eyes. "About what?"

"About the murder of Mrs. Dot Olive," he said.

"You'll have to pardon me. Recent events have got *me* questioning everything," she said, walking through the doors toward the pool. "Especially whether Mr. Berry and I still want to rent here."

They'd just moved in. Then Eric turned to me, "Cassie," he said, "thanks for not sleuthing. It's the only thing going right today."

"I understand," I said.

He flashed me a smile before retreating through the door.

I walked back to the concierge desk and there was no sign of Mr. Berry yet, but there was a fax from Royce:

Dear Cassie,

Just when I thought everything was going swimmingly at the Parkstone. I am struck by this terrifying news. Mrs. Dot Olive was a fine member of the luxurious Parkstone community and to hear that someone had it in for her is maddening! Please make sure the detectives have all the information they need to solve this case. I know you solved the last three murders, but please don't dip your toes in this one. I will fear for the safety of every Parkstonian until the murderer is caught.

I assume the investigation with be underway at the pool. To accommodate such matters, the pool will be closed for the good portion of next week, effective immediately.

Royce Baxter

I folded the fax and placed it in my pocket. A week without the pool was going to be dreadfully long for most Parkstonians.

Chapter 3

Ping! The elevator door opened and Mr. Berry walked out, carrying the vase, which had spilled slightly on his dapper yellow button-down shirt and his blue and gray checkered tweed blazer. *Mr. Berry had a good sense of style*, I thought, *especially his neat navy colored boat shoes*! They looked worn and made his entire ensemble appear more casual.

"Any luck?" he said. "I checked all six floors and no sign of my Evelyn." He placed the vase back on the concierge desk with a thud and an exhausted sigh.

"She was in the sauna," I said. "I guess she skipped swim club for a little R&R. She's corroborating with the detectives now."

"Well, what am I to do?" he said. "I was just trying to have a quiet morning reading in the library. But I sensed trouble was brewing when I didn't hear back from her."

"Well, we've got to stay away from the pool area," I said. "But the questioning shouldn't take very long." And just then I had an idea for sleuthing. I'd make some lemonade and bring the pitcher up to the rooftop for the detectives and those residents being interrogated. *Sleuthing was always refreshing.*

Mr. Berry went to the machine for a second cup of coffee. "I'll wait for Evelyn here," he said. "I can't imagine it will take too long. And I guess I don't really have a choice."

"At least she'll be so happy with the Stargazer lilies when she gets back," I said, glad that at least something had worked out.

Mr. Berry grinned.

I went to the kitchen and made some lemonade and headed back up to the rooftop pool. It was a hot day, and I imagined the detectives could use a cold beverage. I gave a glass of lemonade to Detective Williams and one to Detective Brown. Out of the corner of my eye I saw Eric still interviewing Mrs. Berry, who looked very glamourous wearing a bright glossy lipstick, a floppy straw hat and a black one-piece swimsuit. In truth, Mrs. Berry looked too fashionable to be mixed up in a murder investigation.

I walked along the edge of the pool. I'd have to let the pool cleaners know we'd need the pool cleaned before it could be re-opened to residents. I reminded myself to call them today. I took a deep breath. The air felt crisp. I exhaled swiftly. *Think. How was Mrs. Olive murdered?* The light blue water lapped along the sides of the pool as the detectives combed the water with the cleaning net, looking for clues. I looked to the side and saw them moving Mrs. Olive's plump body onto the stretcher. She was a tint of blue. Her wet curly hair was glued to the sides of her face. It appeared as though she'd been in the pool. So much for thinking swim club was a vacation.

I walked along the pool to the clubhouse and saw two blueberry cupcakes short of a dozen on a paper plate. The cupcakes must have been the ones Mrs. Olive promised Mrs. Kemper if she swam in the pool. That must have meant that Mrs. Kemper was most likely here this morning! I added her to my suspect list. Mrs. Kemper, Mrs. Berry, and Harold Eager, were now all suspects.

Moments later, I heard footsteps behind me. I jumped. It was Eric. "Cassie, what do you think you're doing?"

"Lemonade?" I said, holding up the tray of glasses.

"No," he said seriously. "It's hot out here, but I don't need lemonade, and neither do the other detectives—or residents."

"But they might *like* some," I said, smiling. "Any progress on the case?"

"That's confidential information, Ms. Hall," he said. "But you look great. I like that dress."

I blushed in the heat. Maybe he was trying to charm me in hopes I'd forget about the case, but that wasn't going to happen. I looked at the dress, and said, "It's nothing." Just a very expensive Laundry dress that took me hours to choose and courage to wear, and then Moola had to go and shake her wet fur all over it.

"The guys will be over here soon to fingerprint the glass and cupcake plate, and everything else," he said. "So it's probably best if you leave the crime scene. I wouldn't want you to be accidentally incriminated.'"

"Okay," I said. "I'll go back to the concierge desk, and see how I can be of use there."

Eric smiled. "I'll let you know when I have an update."

I walked back along the pool. I wanted nothing more than to stay on the rooftop and pass out lemonade and overhear conversations. A part of me thought about taking the watering can and start watering the plum trees as an excuse just to be at the crime scene. Any excuse to be on the rooftop. But I'd promised Eric, and I was really going to do my best to stay out of this case.

I headed back to the lobby. There'd be something else to sleuth.

*****

Mr. Berry was still sitting on the velvet plush chairs and looking nervous. What was he so worried about? Mrs. Berry's questioning would probably be over shortly. And I don't think she had a motive. Of course, her alibi was that she was in the sauna, but no one could vouch for her. I still thought she was probably innocent.

Mr. Berry spoke up. "We moved here to downsize," he said. "Not to get sized up by detectives. My wife and I are very reputable, upstanding citizens in the community."

"Please don't worry, Mr. Berry," I said. "Mrs. Berry will be here shortly. And I'm sure there's nothing to worry about. Lemonade?"

"Gladly," he said. "You know we heard her talking."

"Who?" I said.

"Mrs. Olive," he said. "Last night."

Mr. Berry had evidence. This was great. "Where?"

"Why we live right next to her," he said. "And she was talking loudly on her phone. We couldn't understand what she was saying. Couldn't hear that well even if I wanted to. But she sure was upset."

Then that reminded me. Mrs. Olive's apartment, which she'd been kicked out of temporarily because of the water leak. There may be some worthwhile evidence in her apartment. I'd have to get there before the detectives did. I grabbed my ring of concierge keys.

I said goodbye to Mr. Berry, who seemed in better spirits now. I took the elevator to apartment 704 and let myself in, carefully shutting the door behind me.

Mrs. Dot Olive's apartment was well-organized. Especially the living room. There were inspirational quotes like, "Hang In There" and "The Poolside is Your Best Side." This last one was obviously not true. Then there was a *Rocky Lakes* DVD on the shelf next to her large flat screen TV. I picked it up and inspected the smiling cast on the back. There were the parents—Mr.

and Mrs. Moore, three college-aged children and a Labrador dog named Nestle. The show was set in the Rocky Mountains, and chronicled the adventures of Mallory Moore and her group of twenty-something friends living there. I'd never actually seen the movie though, because I was too young when it came out in theaters. But if it was one of Mrs. Olive's favorite movies, I'd have to watch it. The more I knew about Mrs. Olive, the better chance I had of solving the case.

Then I walked to the bathroom to check on the leak. Gray plastic buckets were filled with water, but it looked like the ceiling leak had stopped. I thought about where the leak had started above her apartment. That would be apartment 804—the Rhodes' apartment! I'd check in with them later to see how their apartment had faired.

My phone was ringing. I took it out of my dress pocket. It was Eric. *Great.* He always knew when I was sleuthing. From what I could hear over the phone, it sounded like the crime scene was busy. "Cassie," he said, "we're going to need Mrs. Olive's apartment number. Half the guys are going to move the investigation to her apartment and see what evidence we can find there. What's the number?"

I put back the *Rocky Lakes* DVD. Could I stall? Not really. I knew every resident's apartment number off the top of my head and Eric knew that. "It's apartment 704."

"Great. I'm sending the guys there now," he said. "How's everything at the concierge desk?"

"At the concierge desk?" I said. "Things couldn't be better." It's just that I wasn't exactly there. I quickly hung up with Eric and quietly walked out of Mrs. Olive's apartment. I heard the elevator door open—ping——just as I was locking the door. That must be the detectives. I turned quickly in the opposite direction. I'd take the stairs.

*****

Back at the concierge desk, Mr. and Mrs. Berry were reunited and talking closely on the velvet chairs in the near end of the lobby with the flowers between them. I took the *"Will be back shortly sign,"* off of the desk. I was back.

Mr. Gillrot was the first resident to approach the desk. I was sure he was going to ask about the theater tickets.

"Did I hear that right?" he said. "Another murder? At the upscale Parkstone?"

"You heard correctly," I said, wishing there was some way I could have prevented the murder. If today had been my day off I'd have been at the swim club and I could have prevented any disagreements that would have occurred.

"That swim team was trouble," he said. "I knew it ever since you were passing out those Parkstone swim caps. I don't need goggles to see perfectly clear that there was something menacing about that swim club, and maybe about Mrs. Olive herself."

Oh, for heavens' sake! Mrs. Olive was the sweetest. Where did Mr. Gillrot, the most disgruntled tenant get away with calling the swim club menacing? At least, Mrs. Olive's life seemed straightforward, full of *Rocky Lakes* melodrama and inspirational quotes.

"She ran into me in the hallway on the rooftop floor the other day, and basically cornered me and tried to cajole me into joining the swim club," he said. "I don't want to belong to a club. Especially one that involved wearing a bathing suit and spending time outdoors. I'd rather join the bridge club. And that's saying a lot."

"Well, I'm sure she understood," I said.

"You'd think," he said, "but no. She threw some inspirational quotes my way like 'swim toward your goals' and I said, 'I'd rather drown.'"

Well, Mr. Gillrot had some strong opinions of Mrs. Dot Olive and swim club. "If you don't want to join swim club," I said, "then there are plenty of other clubs to join."

"You're telling me!" he said, walking toward the elevators.

Then the Berrys who'd been glancing over at the concierge desk while I was talking with Mr. Gillrot, approached.

Mrs. Berry spoke up first, gushing over her new bouquet of flowers. Then the conversation turned serious. "I told the detectives everything I know," she said. "I had the best of intentions going to swim club this morning, but I left my phone on a chaise. I even told Mr. Berry that's where he could find me. But when I realized only Mrs. Kemper was there eating a blueberry cupcake Dot had made for her, I figured I'd check out the sauna while I waited for Dot. What's swim club without the leader? And, well, the sauna was so great, I didn't want to leave."

"I think it's our best amenity here at the Parkstone," I said.

"Oh, and I can see why," Mrs. Berry gushed. "It was a great detox. And I'm much more relaxed. Except for the whole murder thing."

"So you never saw Mrs. Olive at the pool this morning?" I said, thinking that was odd.

"Nope," she said. "Only Mrs. Kemper did. She was eating a cupcake, which I believe was from Dot."

"Do you remember anything else about the pool area that looked suspicious?"

She squinted her eyes and thought about it a while before saying, "Not really. Except. Well, I did *hear* something suspicious."

"And what was that?" I said, hoping Mrs. Berry might have a clue important to the case.

"It was a scraping noise," she said.

A scraping noise? There wasn't anything I knew of off the top of my head that would have caused that noise.

She continued, "It was coming from the clearing behind the club house."

There wasn't much back there except a game of corn hole and a grill. I decided I'd investigate that later. Right now, it was just good that Mrs. Berry was safe. "Thanks for cooperating with the detectives. If there's anything I can do to make your time at Parkstone more convenient and luxurious, let me know."

She began to walk away and then turned around. "There's one more thing."

This piqued my interest. "Yes?"

"The cabana," she said. "One of the poles holding it up was at an angle. It was leaning as if it had been pushed to the side."

I had no explanation for that either. "If you remember anything else, you know where to find me."

She took Mr. Berry's hand. "Now, let's go before the detectives ask me about the suspicious sound or the dented cabana!"

He accepted her hand. "Gladly."

As they walked away from the concierge desk, the elevator door opened and out walked Mrs. Canterbury, holding a chocolate cake. "Dear," she said, placing the chocolate cake on the concierge desk, "I thought you might need something sweet to counter all the sour moods and salty comments."

"Mrs. Canterbury," I said, "You're the best."

"A slice of decadence," she said, placing a slice of cake on a plate. "It's a chocolate olive oil cake with rosewater ganache."

The cake was so spongy and delicious. I loved it, especially the chocolate ganache. Then I had an idea. "Mrs. Canterbury," I said, "You're brilliant! I have an idea. Eric and I have been looking for a wedding cake. We have an appointment at Capitol Cakes next week, but I think I'll cancel it because this is the perfect cake!"

"I'll send you the recipe," she said, clasping her hands together.

"And then the caterers can make the cake," I said. "It's perfect! I'll let Eric know."

Then the elevator door opened. Eric walked out flanked by his partner Detective Williams. He was holding bags of evidence.

"Eric," I said, motioning him to come over to the desk.

"Cassie, I need to get back to the station," he said, looking distraught.

"It's about our wedding cake," I said.

He walked over swiftly. "I have a minute."

"This should be our wedding cake," I said, handing him a forkful of the chocolate spongy dessert. "Convinced?"

"Mrs. Canterbury," he said. "Are you the genius behind our wedding cake?"

She blushed. "Oh, you two are going to have such a good life together. My finding this recipe was just the icing on the cake."

And after the cake, the next stage of life for Eric and me would be wedded bliss. We had been meant to be together ever since college, and I didn't see that changing anytime soon. But first there was a more pressing task at hand—I'd have to cancel our wedding cake tasting appointment at Washington D.C.'s posh Capitol Cakes, *and* we had a murder to solve.

Chapter 4

That night I decided against sleuthing the rooftop crime scene. There was yellow caution tape all around the pool area, the chaises, the clubhouse and the collapsed cabana. And there were motion detector lights on the rooftop, so I figured I'd be sure to be found out.

Instead, I decided to watch *Rocky Lakes* on Netflix. I changed out of my hot pink Laundry dress. I was still upset that that Chihuahua Moola had shaken her wet fur all over it. I slipped into my luxurious Derek Rose tapered lounge pants and a cotton t-shirt that Eric had given me for Valentine's Day last year, along with a pastel pink floral print robe. I settled in with a bowl of popcorn and a diet Peach Snapple Iced Tea. Except for the murder, life was grand!

Eric sent me a text message saying he'd be over later. I started watching *Rocky Lakes* and I was hooked. The lines were cheesy in the best way possible, the characters were interesting, and it was set against the backdrop of the Rocky Mountains. The main character named Mallory Moore was my favorite. She was gorgeous and wore a cowgirl hat, cowgirl boots and lots of denim. There was something very familiar about her. It was almost as if I knew her. That Midwestern accent. That easygoing smile. I couldn't quite put my finger on it. I retreated to the kitchen for more popcorn.

I listened to her voice as I poured the popcorn and it just sounded so familiar. Mallory was explaining why a date she'd gone on had gone awry. What was it about her voice?

I carried the bowl back to the living room when Mallory said, "Fat chance of seeing him again!" and cackled. Chills ran up my arms. All of a sudden, I felt like I was at swim club. I dropped the bowl of popcorn. That voice and cackle sounded familiar because it *was* familiar. It was the voice of Mrs. Dot Olive!

The character kept talking and I stared at the screen. I could see it now. Mrs. Olive was a lot plumper now, but in her younger years she was the gorgeous starlet who'd played Mallory Moore in *Rocky Lakes*. I couldn't believe it! She cackled again. There was no mistaking it now. It was the Parkstone's very own Dot Olive. I did a quick Google search and found the IMDB account for Dot Olive, and scrolled down to the *Rocky Lakes* listing. There she was listed as playing Mallory Moore. They noted that Dot Olive was originally from Colorado and was characterized as having a cowgirl cackle and drawl. Parkstone had its very own starlet and we never knew it!

Just then there was a loud knock at the door.

I screamed. I was so caught up in unraveling this mystery that even a knock at the door was jarring. The knocking grew louder. "Cassie, are you okay in there?"

It was Eric's voice. I rushed to the door, and opened it. Then we both looked at each other and said, "You'll never guess what I found."

Then we both said, "You first."

I opened the door more. "Come in," I said. "You won't believe it." Then I told him about how Mrs. Dot Olive was the actress who'd played Mallory Moore on *Rocky Lakes*.

"I see that you know," he said. "It's almost a soap opera. My cousin used to love it."

"Well," I said, "I don't think anyone knew it, but the show's leading lady lived under this roof."

"So, how could that be important to the case?" he said, reaching for some popcorn.

"I don't know yet," I said, "but if there's someone living here who knew that about Dot, and didn't like her because of it, then we have motive."

"That seems like a longshot, but if it turns up anything, let me know," he said. "I've got some news, too. The guys combed the clearing near the poolside, and we found a size eleven boat shoe imprint that we traced along the pool and it stopped at the body. There's only trauma to her forehead, so we think she was pushed from behind, and hit her head on the cement."

"Poor Mrs. Olive!" I said. That sounded horrible.

"We're almost certain that whoever was wearing these boat shoes is our killer. Do you know of any man in the building who wears that type of shoe?"

I thought about it. Not that I knew of. Most men in the building wore loafers, or wing tips. Then I remembered something. "I think I know who those footprints belong to," I said. "But if I tell you, do you promise I can go along for the interrogation?"

Eric looked frustrated. "Cassie, you always find a way to sneak your way into an investigation."

I smiled, knowing he'd give in. "Great. This morning, Mr. Berry was wearing navy blue boat shoes," I said. "I noticed them in the lobby. *And* he told me he hadn't been to the pool this morning." Mr. Berry was a liar at best, and a killer at worst.

Eric shook his head. "These footprints were fresh." He paused. "I'm going...I mean, we're going to interrogate him now."

I cinched my robe around me, and slipped out of my fluffy slippers and into my high heel peep toe shoes. I was now in investigation mode.

Eric and I rode the elevator to the fifth floor. We knocked on apartment door 706, and Mrs. Berry answered the door.

"Oh, Cassie, isn't it sweet of you to check up on me," she said. Then she called into the other room. "Walter, Cassie and her fiancé Detective Peters are here to see us."

I hated to dash her hopes for our visit, but the least amount of time spent on pleasantries, the quicker we could solve Mrs. Olive's death. Mr. Berry joined his wife.

Mrs. Berry continued, "You know, I really am feeling fine today. I was shaken up by Dot's death—and the interrogation, which I still think was a trite unnecessary. But I was happy to help with the case."

"The case," Eric said, "is exactly what brings us here tonight."

"And on short notice," Mrs. Berry said, giving my robe a once over.

"Precisely," I said.

Eric cleared his throat. "There were footprints of a men's size eleven boat shoe found at the scene of the crime. The footprints were found poolside leading up to the body."

Then I spoke up. "If your boat shoes were the culprit, then we need to know."

Mr. Berry looked baffled. "How did this happen? You're making a mistake."

Mrs. Berry put her hands over her mouth. "Walter, did you harm Mrs. Olive?"

"No, no, of course not," he said.

"Then do you mind if we come in and compare your shoe to the footprints found at the scene?"

"Why, of course I mind, but that's not going to stop you, is it?" he said.

Mrs. Berry looked confused. "So, dear, you *were* at the pool this morning?"

"Come in, and shut the door," Mr. Berry said. "I can make this easy on everyone."

I shuffled in but didn't exactly feel comforted considering he could be the killer.

*****

We all sat in the large armchairs in the Berry's living room. Considering they'd just moved into the Parkstone a couple of days ago, their apartment was nearly all unpacked. There were even some paintings on the walls—vibrant watercolors, and etchings. There was a set of tea cups on the coffee table, which Mrs. Berry moved to the side table. "Mr. Berry and I were just enjoying some evening green tea," she said. "Care for any?"

Eric and I declined. We still didn't trust that Mr. Berry wasn't the killer.

He spoke calmly. "This morning, Mrs. Berry said she was going to the pool for swim club, and asked if I wanted to join," he said.

She chimed in, "I knew you'd say no. You haven't swam in years."

"Right," he said, "but I went up to the pool after I got my coffee to see how it was going for you. But when I get up there, the rooftop was as hot as a desert and as vacant as one too. Not a soul except for a woman lying face down in the grass under the cabana—a woman, who, at that time, I didn't know was Mrs. Olive."

"Oh, dear," Mrs. Berry said, "You could have witnessed a murder!"

"I saw the figure lying down, and I just thought it was a little odd she wasn't tanning on one of the chaises. And why wasn't the cabana standing up? So I walked up to the figure, and when she didn't move, I didn't know what to do. I thought maybe she'd fallen asleep under the cabana and it had just blown over in the wind."

It was beginning to make sense. He continued, "I didn't think she was dead. It wasn't until you told me later, Cassie, that I got to thinking that maybe the dead person and the person I saw laying on the grass were one and the same."

"You understand this places you at the scene of the crime, don't you?" Eric said.

"Yes, he said. "I admit I was there. But I was looking for Evelyn. I didn't harm Mrs. Olive."

"And what time were you there?"

"Difficult to say exactly," he said, "but probably around 10:30."

Eric gave me an affirming look and said, "I think that's enough for tonight." Then he looked at Mr. Berry. "We'll need to confiscate your boat shoes." And to Mrs. Berry, he said, "Hopefully, next time we'll see you under better circumstances."

"Really," she said, "anything we can do to help. And I think between my interrogation this morning and this interrogation tonight, we've helped enough."

Mr. Berry walked out of the bedroom carrying his boat shoes, which Eric sealed in a plastic bag.

"I'll have to get you new boat shoes," Mrs. Berry said, wrapping her arms around Mr. Berry, and giving Eric and me a sideways grimace.

I thought about men's summer shoes. There were a lot to choose from: Sperry, L.L. Bean or Crocs. Eric and I were going on vacation to the eastern shore in two weeks. I'd already bought flip flops for myself and for him a pair of leather sport sandals, for walking along the beach. We walked back down the hallway to my apartment, with the sandals sealed as evidence. I couldn't wait to solve this murder so sunscreen and days at the beach would be my top concern.

Back at my apartment, I took off my heels and slipped into my fluffy slippers. "Do you believe him?" I said to Eric, who looked like he wanted to get back to the station.

"I think he's telling the truth," he said. "It's completely plausible what he said. He doesn't have a motive for killing Mrs. Olive, and most likely didn't even know that was her. What's kind of strange is that he didn't tell his wife that he went to check on her and that he was at the pool that morning."

"Maybe he thought she would think it was petty?"

"Maybe," Eric said, sounding unconvinced. "It's just something to keep in mind." He paused. "For now, we've got what we wanted—the size eleven boat shoes to place him at the scene."

I smiled. "I think I should go on more interrogations."

He smiled back. "You would say that."

Eric headed back to the station and I grabbed the controls to watch the rest of *Rocky Lakes*.

Just who was Dot Olive and who wanted her head?

*****

The next day, I stood at the concierge desk flipping though my lilac-colored wedding checklist planner that I kept in a drawer behind the concierge desk. That way, when I had some down time—which was quit frequent during the summer because all the guests vacationed—I could get ready for Eric's and my wedding. The lobby was quiet and it didn't appear as though residents needed me for anything at the moment, and our wedding would be here before we knew it.

I could cross *"choose wedding cake"* off the list, because Mrs. Canterbury's recipe for the chocolate cake with rosewater ganache was already voted the delicious winner. I couldn't wait to tell the caterers. I'd have to double check with them first, so I added that to the list. Then there was also the photographer for the engagement photos, and choosing the location. How fun it would be to scope out the Parkstone for the perfect photo engagement spot!

And most importantly, we'd have to choose a date; Eric and I couldn't agree on one. He thought Valentine's Day would be great because that's when he'd proposed. I agreed that day was lovely, but I was hoping to avoid, in the way I automatically duck when I see Mr. Gillrot, a wedding on a major holiday. I hadn't told him yet, but I was thinking more along the lines of April.

Yes, that would be the perfect time of year to get married. It would be crisp and warm, not hot and humid like it is now, in the dead of summer.

Then I began working on the guest list. Mrs. Canterbury was at the top. And I was thinking we could invite Mr. Harold Eager, too. As long as he wasn't the murderer! Then I crossed out "*wedding guest list*" and wrote, "*suspect list*." Instead of narrowing the guest list, I was making a suspect list—and a pretty extensive one at that.

There was Harold Eager, Mr. Berry, Mrs. Kemper, and Mary Chris. And there could be more I'd discover once I got busy sleuthing.

Just then, I saw Mr. Eager approach the concierge desk. I had to think quickly. I folded the paper and put it in the pocket of my Willow and Clay floral midi dress. I put away the lilac wedding agenda, too. It was time to sleuth.

"I'm going to play croquet," said Mr. Eager, with a pouch of croquet clubs carried on his shoulders. "Mr.

Berry should be meeting me out there shortly. It's very nice to have him and Mrs. Berry in the building."

I agreed. But I needed to know why Mr. Eager was at the pool yesterday morning when Mrs. Olive, the Parkstone's starlet, was killed. I was certain that towel was his on the chaise, mainly because it was dry and he never went in the water.

"I can't believe what happened to Mrs. Olive," I said, placing a hand over my forehead for dramatic effect. I'd really been inspired by *Rocky Lakes*. I could use acting skills of my own.

"Why yes, it's horrible, but why are you talking to me about it?" he said. "I really should get out to the croquet court."

The croquet court was on the far end of the courtyard and was very popular amongst the residents looking for a leisurely, yet competitive sport.

"It's just that it's strange you were at the pool yesterday morning," I said, "and didn't mention it to detectives."

"How do you know that?" he said.

"Which one?" I said, knowing I'd caught him in his croquet game tracks. "I know you were at the pool because there was a dry towel on the last chaise. And I asked Eric, and he said you denied being at the pool."

"Because I was trying to avoid *this*," he said, angrily huffing and puffing. His mood had changed as quickly as a croquet swing. "Your snooping around Cassie isn't going to solve anything."

"If you have nothing to hide," I said, "then why don't you be forthright in telling me why you were at the pool?"

"What do you mean?" he said. "I was there because of swim club. It's just that when I showed up, no one was there. And to be honest, I was looking for an excuse to skip it anyway, so I left." He paused. "Must have forgotten my towel on the chaise."

I eyed him suspiciously. That sounded as though it could be the truth. Then I felt as though I'd come across too strong. I changed from sleuth to concierge mode. "I'm very sorry to hear that Mr. Eager," I said. "I assure you the detectives have the situation under control, and the killer will be caught soon. Please enjoy your day on the croquet court with Mr. Berry."

"Don't tell Mr. Berry," he said, "but I have a few tricks up my sleeve." He paused. "And you and your fiancé Eric should know I'd much rather hit a ball through wickets, than off a plump swim club leader! I'm staying out of the investigation."

Unless we needed his account of events from that morning, I thought. "Good to know," I said, as I watched him walk through the courtyard doors. Jet-Setter and Cashmere leapt off the concierge desk with all the excitement. "Nothing going on here," I said, as they followed me to the coffee station. It looked like I was interrogating the wrong suspect. I made a cup of dark roast coffee and sat back behind the concierge desk. Later that night, I'd have to be sure to tell my mom about Mrs. Dot Olive starring in the *Rocky Lakes* movie. Seeing as how it was set in Colorado, she might know a thing or two about it that could be helpful to the case.

Chapter 5

After an hour passed, I decided to take a walk to the croquet court in the courtyard. I was carrying a serving tray of lemonade. Mr. Eager and Mr. Berry looked in good spirits, laughing at what I guessed were pleasantries.

"Well, how are you, Cassie?" Mr. Eager said.

I smiled. "Happy to see the game is going so well," I said. "Lemonade?"

When I walked through the courtyard I'd seen Mr. Berry and Mr. Eager had picked up a third croquet competitor, Mr. Gillrot, who was so ornery I was surprised he was capable of sportsmanship.

The croquet court was well manicured, and as I looked up at the recently clipped topiary looming above us, and the pink and red crab apple trees, I thought what a perfect place to work and live, except for the humidity. I set the tray of lemonade on a nearby white wrought iron table, and picked up a mallet that was resting on the side of the court.

"Taking a break from investigating the crime?" Mr. Eager said.

"What makes you assume I was investigating? I said, practicing my swing on the lawn.

Mr. Gillrot cleared his throat. "You investigate the Parkstone crimes like these birds take to the crabapple trees—always in it unless someone scares you away."

I laughed. For as ill as his disposition was, Mr. Gillrot could be amusing. "Well, I solved the first three crimes," I said coolly. "What makes you think this one would be any different?"

Mr. Gillrot let his head roll to the side. "Because Parkstone killers are getting smarter. Mrs. Olive was secretive, but also the nicest person at the residence. Good luck finding someone who disliked her, let alone wanted to killed her."

"Enough murder talk," Mr. Eager said, motioning toward the first wicket. "You first, Cassie. Walter and Mr. Gillrot and I will need a quick breather. This humidity is murder."

My ears felt hot. "Speaking of which…"

Mr. Gillrot sat up straighter. "Give it up, Cassie."

I continued, "Were any of you privy to Mrs. Olive's whereabouts that morning?" I said. It had occurred to me, that what I needed for the case was information about any scuffles she might have had before she reached the rooftop pool.

Mr. Berry looked over at the lemonade tray. "On second thought, I'll take one of those lemonades." Then more quietly under his breath, "Yes, this could be a while."

Mr. Eager put his hand to his temple. "Now that you mention it, Cassie," he said, "I recall Mary Chris and Mrs. Olive getting into a spat at the pool during the second day of swim club."

My heart quickened. "Really?"

"Yes, you weren't there, but those two got into a real cat fight about just about everything they could have argued about at the pool. Whether diving was allowed while other residents were swimming, whether to play music from Mary Chris' iPod or not. Whether Mary Chris was paying attention to Mrs. Olive's inspirational speech about swimming," he said. "I was exhausted, and I didn't even go in the water."

I made a mental note of Mary Chris. I'd have to add her to the suspect list. I reached into my dress pocket for the folded suspect list, but my pocket was empty. Where was the list? I quickly moved my eyes to search the grounds—the croquet court and the crabapple tree path I'd walked down. I must have looked panicked, but I didn't care. I couldn't let that list get into the wrong hands.

My eyes scanned the lawn. Then my eye caught a glimpse of the edge of a piece of paper. My suspect list was resting on the side of the lawn under the wrought iron table. It must have fallen out of my pocket when I'd bent over to place the lemonade tray on the table.

Just then, I saw Mr. Gillrot's eyes follow mine to the piece of paper. Oh no! If Mr. Gillrot got a hold of the suspect list I'd never hear the end of it. I lunged forward in my peep-toe shoes. I stepped on the folded piece of paper just as Mr. Gillrot lunged forward in his chair and crashed to the floor. I held tight to the list and I put my chin up in the air, triumphant.

"What have you got there?" he said. "Is that a list of who you think did it?"

"Maybe?" I said, placing the folded paper carefully back in my dress pocket. "I guess now you'll never know."

He growled. "Cassie, there's something important on that paper. You couldn't wear a poker face if it were high heel shoes. You make sorting my wines by year, brand and type seem like a piece of chocolate mousse cake."

I was so happy to have the suspect list back. It could have been bad if it had gotten into the wrong hands. I walked to the beginning of the croquet court. I hit the wooden ball through the first wicket, landing my ball with perfect positioning for the second. My croquet skills were as sharp as my killer sense of whodunit. Mr.

Berry and Mr. Gillrot and Mr. Eager played their hand at the game and we went back and forth like that until I got a text message from Eric: *Call me. It's about the case.*

I was so anxious I dropped the phone.

Mr. Gillrot shook his head. "What's gotten into you, Cassie?"

"My hands are unstable, maybe from so much croquet," I said with an unconvincing smile.

"Probably not," he said. "And I know there was important information on that note of yours."

I said goodbye and thanked them for letting me join their game. We exchanged pleasantries, and then I took the lemonade tray and started walking up the hill.

Mr. Gillrot called after me, "Why are you leaving the game now? You were winning." Then I saw him turn to Mr. Berry and say, "Such an odd woman."

Once I was back in the building, I walked to the club room for some privacy to call Eric. He picked up on the first ring.

"Cassie," he said, "there's something strange from the crime scene that I need to tell you about."

"Yes?" I said, so happy to be let in on the secret. From the large bay window in the club room, I could see Mr. Berry, Mr. Gillrot and Mr. Eager continuing to play croquet.

"It's about the swim cap Mrs. Olive was wearing," he said.

"Yes, I know about the swim caps," I said. "Corporate sent us a large box of Parkstone swim caps along with towels for the pool and sauna. Why? Was there something suspicious?"

"Yes," he said. "There were two long, bright red strands of straight hair found in the swim cap she was wearing."

"But Mrs. Olive was a brunette," I said.

"Hence, the mystery," he said. "I figured if I called you, you'd know which resident had that color hair so I'd know who to interrogate. The other thing is, it's dyed."

I thought for a second, watching the croquet players swing the mallets and laugh jovially. "It's from Mrs. Penelope Rhodes," I said. "It must be. She's the only resident with dyed red hair. It's almost the deep red of a sunset. All the other female residents have gray, brown, black or blond hair."

"Well this red head is in for a surprise," he said. "We're going to pay her a visit."

"We?" I said. "Me too?"

"The residents need you as their trusty concierge," he said, "not meddling in their affairs."

"I'm doing this for Mrs. Olive," I said. "She was always so supportive of my personal shopping certificate aspirations," I said. "She convinced me to go for my goals, and dive into my dreams. I owe it to her."

"All right," he said. "Detective Williams and I are heading over there now."

I smiled, and turned to look out the courtyard window. Mr. Gillrot was holding a mallet above Mr. Eager's head! I opened the bay window and called out: "What's gotten into you?" But they weren't within earshot. Mr. Gillrot was now shaking the mallet at Mr. Eager, while Mr. Berry tried to hold him back.

I flung the bay window open. Tucked my dress firmly around my knees and wiggled out of the window and over the hedge in front of it. I grabbed onto the leg of the elephant topiary plants and secured my landing on the ground. I ran as quickly as I could in my peep-toe shoes and shouted, "Mr. Gillrot, stop!"

He turned toward me, just as Mr. Berry wrestled the mallet from his hands and threw it to the croquet court lawn.

Mr. Gillrot was leaning to the sides and stabilizing himself with his hands on his hips.

"What's going on here?" I said, trying to catch my breath. "The detectives will be here within minutes. So if there's anything else I need to report…"

"He started it!" Mr. Gillrot said, pointing a finger at Mr. Eager. "And he's the one who killed Mrs. Olive!"

"What makes you say that?" I said, confused, although Mr. Eager *was* on my suspect list. I also thought Mr. Gillrot said he was staying out of the case.

"There's just something very suspicious about him," Mr. Gillrot said. "Suspicion leads to murder."

Mr. Eager turned toward me. "The detectives are going to be here?" he said.

"Yes," I said. "They're probably walking through the valet doors as we speak."

"Great," he said.

"What are you so happy about?" Mr. Gillrot said.

"I think I'm done with croquet for today," Mr. Berry said. "Gentleman." He nodded at the men and walked up the courtyard path to the building.

I didn't blame him. Mr. Eager continued, "If you don't mind, Cassie, I'd like to talk to the detectives. There's something else I know that might be useful to solving the case."

Mr. Gillrot dug his loafer into the grass. "Convenient. All too convenient."

"Please, gentleman," I said, "preserve the croquet court and watch your language. Mr. Eager, let's see if the detectives are here."

As we walked up the courtyard's stone path, I noticed that my nametag was slightly askew on my midi floral dress after I'd crawled out of the club room window.

I adjusted the clip of my concierge badge, which I pictured as reading, "*Cassie Hall, Concierge Sleuth.*"

*****

Once we were in the lobby, I saw Eric and Detective Williams standing in the far end. "Apartment number for Mrs. Penelope Rhodes?" Eric said.

Mr. Eager gasped. "Mrs. Rhodes!"

"They just want to ask her a few questions," I said. He nodded and said, "She seems so pleasant."

Eric gave me a look like, *What's he doing here?* I smiled and said, "There's something Mr. Eager would like to say about the crime."

"Great," he said. "Can it wait? I'd love to get the Rhodes' interrogation done first."

I nodded. "Mr. Eager, we'll be right back," I said. "Don't forget what you were going to tell us."

"That's not possible," he said. "Now that I remembered it."

Eric, Detective Williams and I took the elevator to the eighth floor in silence. I wanted to talk Eric's ear off about the case, but knew better than to jeopardize my chance of getting to tag along. The Rhodes' had a really inviting wreath on their door with dried yellow and pink flowers on it and a large lavender colored bow. I hated to deliver the surprise of an interrogation.

Eric knocked loudly on the door. Mr. Rhodes answered on the second knock. "Hello, detective," he said, his eyes scurrying from each one of us to the next. "Cassie, can I help you?"

Eric spoke up first. "We're here to see your wife, Penelope. May we come in?"

"Of course," Mr. Rhodes said, as he pulled their Chihuahua Moola, who was jumping uncontrollably, to the side of the hallway. "Excuse the mess, we had a leak here the other day, and we're still cleaning up from it."

Mrs. Rhodes stood in the kitchen with a paper towel and pretended to wipe something from the counter, then she smiled and said, "Because picking up spills shouldn't be a pill."

Then she laughed and tossed the paper towel. "I'm practicing for my *Spark Clean* commercial. I'm convinced I'm going to get the part."

It must be interesting to have the life of a commercial actress. *I guess the leak gave her a lot of practice*, I thought. I'd almost forgotten that this was the apartment above the victim's—Mrs. Olive's, apartment. "Did you know Mrs. Olive well?" I said.

Eric shot me glance.

Mr. Rhodes shook his head. "I knew her in passing," he said. "She was always very busy. Always seemed in a rush to wherever she was going."

Mrs. Penelope Rhodes emerged from the kitchen wiping her hands on her apron. "Besides practicing for my audition, I was just making lunch. Can I make you something?" she said to the detectives.

"No thank you," Eric said. "We have a couple of questions to ask you." He took the swim cap sealed in a plastic bag out of his pocket. "Is this yours?"

"How could I tell? All the Parkstone swim caps look the same. Right, Cassie?"

"Right," I said, wondering how her swim cap had ended up on Mrs. Olive's head. If Mrs. Rhodes was the killer, did she kill Mrs. Olive and then switch swim caps? But what would she gain from that?

Eric continued, "There were two strands of long red hair that seem a match for yours and were found in the the victim's swim cap," he said.

"So that's mine. You found it!" she said exuberantly.

Eric looked solemn. "Before you get too excited about it, you must know this is the one we found on Mrs. Olive's head at the scene of the crime."

"What?!" Mrs. Rhodes said. "So *she's* the one who took it?"

Then I chimed in, "Slow down," I said. "What do you mean she *took* it?"

"You're right, Cassie," Mrs. Rhodes said. "*Stole* it is more like it!"

Eric shook his head. "So the victim stole your swim cap?"

"Yes, the day Mrs. Olive was killed," she said. "I was going to ask for a replacement one. She stole it right out of my locker on the rooftop. How impossibly cruel."

"Did she have a reason for stealing it?" Eric said.

Then Mr. Rhodes—who was trying to contain the high-energy Moola, chimed in. "Should we sit down?"

We all took a seat on the couch near the balcony. A lot of sun was pouring through the window and it made me think of one of the staged photographs in the Parkstone brochures, which were staged to perfection— and were minus the murders.

"I disliked her in the way I dislike salted caramel truffles," she said. "I'm sure they're great, lots of people like them, but I'll always pass on one for a chocolate raspberry truffle instead."

Eric looked bewildered. I decided to speak up. "Did you two ever get into a disagreement?" I said. "At the pool, maybe?"

"If you're asking if I killed her, you're wrong," she said. "If anything, she was out to get me!"

Mr. Rhodes put a hand on his wife's knee. "Sweetheart," he said, "I wouldn't go that far."

"She stole my swim cap, and wore it. She accused me one day of being out to get her," she said. "She even blamed this leak in our apartment on me and was upset that she had to go to the guest suite—as if the plumbing is our problem."

Just then, I glanced around the room, and the entertainment stand with TV and DVDs caught my eye.

I was perusing their DVD collection when I noticed something fascinating: The *Rocky Lakes* DVD! I'd never heard a resident talk about that movie in my life and now here were two residents who owned the movie—one of whom starred in it! Was this more than just a coincidence? Something told me that Mrs. Penelope Rhodes' dislike of Mrs. Olive was greater than that of a salted caramel truffle.

Chapter 6

By the time we got back to the lobby, Mr. Eager was sitting in the near end looking out of the street level window and sipping a cup of coffee. "I thought you'd forgotten about me," he said. "I'm on my second cup of coffee. Good thing it's decaf."

Eric approached the velvet plush chairs and took a seat next to Mr. Eager. "Cassie said you remembered something you think might be pertinent to the crime."

"I can't believe I didn't remember it the day of the murder," he said. "But better late than never. I thought you might like to know I remembered more specifics about the argument I overheard between Mary Chris and Mrs. Olive in the pool the day before the murder."

"Do you know what they were arguing about?" Eric said, as Detective Williams took a seat, intrigued.

"Yes," Mr. Eager said. "Although, I've got to say it sounds trivial. Mrs. Olive was trying to give Mary Chris pointers on her backstroke, and, well, Mary Chris wouldn't have it. She said not everyone needed to be as good a swimmer technically as Mrs. Olive." Then his eyes got bigger and he said. "Then you'll never believe what happened. Mrs. Olive told Mary Chris that her signature fishtail braid had so many knots in it that there was probably a bird living inside, and that she despised birds." Mr. Eager took a deep breath. He put his coffee mug down and gestured wildly with his hands. "And then Mary Chris said to Mrs. Olive, 'Watch out, enough insults and you'll be through.'"

I gasped. I couldn't picture Mary Chris saying such a thing, even to someone she disliked. And I couldn't picture Mrs. Olive saying the birds comment either, even though she was really afraid of them.

I thought back to the day of the murder. I was standing in the rooftop vestibule and I saw Mary Chris on the rooftop that morning, and she said she was there for swim club. It didn't seem like there was bad blood between them.

Eric was taking notes in his notebook. "Thank you, Mr. Eager, this has been very helpful. We'll have a talk with Mary Chris and see if we can straighten things out."

"That sounds great," Mr. Eager said, looking at the empty coffee cup. "I hope it leads to something. And I think that's my last coffee for today."

After Eric was done taking notes in his notebook and Mr. Eager had gone out to the courtyard, Eric turned to me and said, "One more thing that's odd. We found two uncooked hamburger patties in the trash can at the scene of the crime. They were still in the plastic wrap. Who wouldn't have grilled up those patties on such a beautiful day?"

"The killer!" I said. "What if someone planned to grill but then ended up killing Mrs. Olive and needed a quick escape?"

"Exactly," he said.

"Do you have any other clues?" I said, anxious to help with the investigation.

He shook his head. "Not at this time. I wish though. We have a vacation coming up and I want to make sure I can be there with you."

I agreed. The beach would only be fun if the both of us were there. "We better wrap up this case by then!"

"For now, let me know as soon as you see something or remember something suspicious," he said. "And we'll keep piecing clues together at the station."

My next step was to find out who was at the grill. I could rule out our vegetarian residents. Just then, I discovered a suspect who could be ruled out. "Come to think of it, Mary Chris might be in the clear," I said. "She might have exchanged strong words with Mrs. Olive, but I know she's a vegetarian, so she wouldn't have been the one about to grill the hamburger patties."

"We're going to have to interview her anyway," he said. "Those are too strong of words that she said to Mrs. Olive for us to ignore."

"Let's go," I said. "Apartment 703."

We motioned to Detective Williams, who was at the coffee station, to join us at the elevators. He seemed happier after a cup of caffeine.

We took the elevator to Mary Chris' apartment and found her there with her earphones plugged in, about to go to the gym. "Can I help you?" she said slowly, looking surprised.

Eric flashed his detective badge. She let us in and said, "Is this about Dot?"

We nodded. Then Eric said, "If we could have a moment of your time. We'd like to ask you a couple of questions."

"I was just going to the gym," she said. "But it can wait."

She let us into the foyer and to the living room, where we all took a seat on the couch.

Eric opened his notebook. "We've been informed from another resident that you and Mrs. Olive got into a pretty intense disagreement in the pool the other day."

Mary Chris rolled her eyes. "That must have been Mr. Eager. I was upset, and sometimes when we're upset we all say things we don't mean. Mrs. Olive was so nit-picky about everyone's stroke, and I'd really just joined swim club to have fun. Which she was thwarting. But I didn't kill her."

"I know that the day she died I ran into you in the rooftop vestibule," I said. "Were you at swim club that morning before I ran into you?"

Her voice turned stern. "I was *not* at swim club that morning. I had every intention of going, but got a late start, okay? And now thanks to the killer, I have to go work out at the gym instead of the pool. Trust me, this isn't the way I would have it."

And just to confirm that, I said, "And you're a vegetarian, right?"

She laughed. "Yes, but what has that got to do with anything?"

Eric shot me a glance.

"Never mind," I said.

She grimaced. "And I don't want to name names, but Mr. Eager was none too happy with Mrs. Olive himself."

"Oh?" I said.

The tables had turned. She continued, "They got into an arguing match that morning. He seemed perfectly content sun bathing on the chaise, but she *insisted* he go in the pool and face his fears. Mr. Eager was so upset he was shaking his finger at her and said, 'You better let people go at their own pace, or else!'"

Eric looked at me and raised his eyebrows. We'd just got done interviewing Mr. Eager and he had failed to mention this.

Eric closed his notebook and said, "Thank you for your time. This has been very helpful."

She smiled. "And Cassie," she said, "When is the pool going to re-open?"

"In two days, most likely," I said. "Royce and the detectives will make that call."

We still had to get the pool cleaners to clean the pool, and the pool cabana, which had collapsed and needed to be fixed. And then there was the fact that the cement and grassy area were a crime scene and it would be difficult to get over that.

I thought it interesting that Mrs. Olive had had a huge fear of birds, but she was always convincing others to get over their fears.

As we were walking out of Mary Chris' apartment and saying our goodbyes, I thought it would be a good idea to hold a memorial ceremony for Mrs. Olive on the rooftop. Maybe on the day the pool re-opened? We could hold the ceremony at the rooftop's chestnut tree where Mrs. Olive would always hang her towel. I'd ask Royce about it, but was confident he would agree it was a good idea. Maybe gauging by the attendees present, I could deduce more info about the case.

Once in the lobby, Eric said, "Well, we're back at square one."

I shook my head. "It sounds like Mr. Eager and Mrs. Olive got into a heated discussion."

"Does he like hamburgers?" Eric said with a sideways glance.

I headed out toward the courtyard. "We'll have to ask."

Mr. Eager was nowhere to be found in the courtyard. Then we went to his apartment, but he didn't answer. We checked the club room, library, and tenth floor cactus terrace. But he wasn't hiding in those places either.

Eric kissed me and said, "We'll come back later for the Eager interview—part two."

I smiled, thinking, *maybe I will have figured out the mystery by then.*

*****

That afternoon I wrote a letter to Royce updating him on the mystery's latest happenings. The afternoon light set in, and everything was calm. At the Parkstone that was always a sign of approaching mayhem.

Dear Royce,

The detectives are making great strides in the case of Mrs. Dot Olive's death. They have been on the Parkstone premises the past couple of days to conduct interviews. Be assured your trusty concierge has done her best not to meddle. Truth be told, everything at the Parkstone now seems suspicious—even the croquet court!

What are your thoughts on commemorating Mrs. Olive's life in a ceremony near the rooftop's chestnut tree? I can send out invitations and plan for the gathering this weekend. Also, residents are probing: will the pool be open by then?

Cassie Hall

I faxed the letter, which woke up Jet-Setter and Cashmere, who'd been fast asleep at my feet. Mr. Eager then walked through the revolving doors, carrying a box from the Pinecone Bakery that was located through the courtyard, and on the other side of the Parkstone's catwalk.

"Chocolate chip cupcakes with ample frosting," he said. "Would you like to have one?"

I couldn't resist. "They look great," I said.

"I just walked right across the catwalk, over the street, and there's this great bakery there. I'd never been before."

I'd been to the Pinecone bakery plenty of times, but there was just one thing about getting there—the catwalk overlooking the street. It was so high up and each time I set out to go to the bakery, it took me a lot of angst to get over my fear of heights.

Sometimes I'd grip the catwalk's wooden railing all the way across the street. Other times I'd sprint across the catwalk with my eyes nearly closed. If it weren't for my dreadfully horrible fear of heights, I'd go to the bakery more often.

And it never disappointed. I took a bite out of the cupcake. It was delicious and perfect for an afternoon respite.

Jet-Setter and Cashmere nudged the box that was resting on top of the concierge desk. They meowed and looked up at me, wondering if they could have a bite. Pinecone baked goods were loved by all—even fur balls.

Mr. Eager picked the box up off the concierge desk. "At the bakery, they heard about the murder, you know?" he said. "They're all talking about it. Apparently, Mrs. Olive used to go there a lot. Every pastry chef there was asking me how things are going at the Parkstone. They said it was good to see I was alive."

He took another bite out of his cupcake. The bakers' comments weren't surprising. This was our fourth murder after all.

"About Mrs. Olive," I said. "Did she give you a hard time about tanning beside the pool?" I was searching for information.

He grimaced. "All she wanted was to teach Parkstone residents how to swim," he said. "And I'm incorrigible. I'll go at my own pace, which consisted of me outside the pool on a chaise. But I wasn't there that morning, and I didn't kill Mrs. Olive."

Then he stepped away from the concierge desk in a huff. "And I want that to be the end of it. If you don't mind, I'm going to enjoy these cupcakes outside in the courtyard, because the pool is still closed."

I looked at my half-eaten chocolate chip frosting cupcake. I thought about the Pinecone Bakery across the courtyard catwalk. If Mrs. Olive was a frequent customer, that might be a good place to investigate.

*****

That night I called my mom, who would be visiting soon. I had the *Rocky Lakes* movie on in the background in case I picked up on anything from the movie that could help solve the case. My mom answered on the first ring. "I've been worried about you!" she said. "I got your text that there's been another murder at the Parkstone."

"Yes," I said. "Our resident Mrs. Dot Olive was killed on the rooftop pool. Of all the places, one of the most luxurious amenities at the Parkstone."

"Dot Olive?" she said. "*The* Dot Olive? Or Mallory Moore, I should say."

"That's the one," I said.

"She was such a great actress," my mom said in disbelief. "I know her from *Rocky Lakes*. She was very famous back in the day."

"Yes, that's her," I said. "I knew her voice sounded familiar when I was watching *Rocky Lakes* the other night, even though she looks very different than her character back then. But before that, she'd been a resident here a long time and I had no idea she was a leading lady."

"Well, she must look different," my mom said. "That movie is from nearly thirty years ago! How do *you* remember it? You were too young to watch that drama when it first came out."

"I've been investigating the crime," I said. "And the other night, I discovered Dot Olive was a famous movie star. I'm trying to find out whether there could be a connection to her previous life as an actress and someone here at the Parkstone."

"Well, I can tell you there were a lot of rocky moments on set," my mom said. "I remember reading that a fire was started on set on their first day of filming. There was a lot of damage, and many of the crew said they thought it was arson."

This was very interesting. She continued, "The fire was set in Dot Olive's trailer, but since it was up in the Rocky Mountains, and there was a lot of firewood and kindle around, they chalked it up to a brush fire."

"But you think it could have been intentional?"

"A lot of people did," she said. "It was all over the news."

I knew I was going to investigate that. She continued, "And I've got to say I'm not happy that you're investigating another crime. A vicious person who's killed someone will kill again. You want to stay as far away from that as possible."

"I'm fine, Mom," I said. "Eric is dissuading me from investigating the crime, too. So between the two of you I've been warned that it's a bad idea."

"Exactly," she said. "How is Eric? Have you two set a wedding date yet?"

"The location is the Parkstone," I said. "Which you know, but the date hasn't been set." Eric still wanted a Valentine's Day wedding, and I was hoping for spring. I paused. "We did choose the cake though. It's a recipe from a resident baker, who said it would be easy for the caterers to make."

"Great! So now you just need to set a date, get a photographer, choose engagement photo locations, hire a band, and send out invitations."

My head hurt. Solving the murder sounded easier than planning a wedding.

"I'll talk with Eric about the date and start thinking about everything else, too."

"Something tells me if you weren't spending so much time investigating, you'd have had your wedding planned by now."

That was true, but a lot of this depended on Eric, too. And he was busy working to solve the crime also.

I said goodbye to my mom and wished her safe travels for her visit to Parkstone. I also promised to let her know the wedding date, and any updates in the case. Then I turned the volume up on *Rocky Lakes* and sat at my computer. I was in full investigation mode. I had articles to read about the arson on the set.

It turned out my mom was right about the fire on the set of the *Rocky Lakes* movie. In fact, it was specifically set at Dot Olive's trailer, which made me think it was personal. Was the culprit who was out to get her then the same killer as now? I looked at the cast list; there were Dot's parents, two younger sisters, a dog named Brady and a love interest. None of the actors' names looked familiar. I was wondering if there was another famous person from the *Rocky Lakes* cast living under the Parkstone roof. But there didn't seem to be.

Then I turned to the television, just as Mrs. Olive's character responded to her suitor's confession that he'd fallen out of love: "You wouldn't have swum through Lake Granby to me unless you were. Madly."

Then he shook his head and eventually collapsed into her embrace. Dot was quit the wielder of power on-screen. I tried to imagine her life before she died. She seemed to love living at the extravagant Parkstone; I knew that, because she would tell me often. She frequently made dinners for the concierges and doted on them with gifts. But I wasn't sure she ever got along with the residents. I thought about it some more and was convinced the murderer was not only someone at swim club, but someone who'd held a grudge that might have been in connection with *Rocky Lakes*.

Chapter 7

The next morning, before my shift started, I walked through the courtyard and approached the catwalk to Pinecone Bakery. My breathing quickened. My hands trembled and were clammy, but not from the humidity. My jittery nerves were in full force and I hadn't even started walking over the street.

I decided to look at the walkway to calm my fear of heights. The catwalk looked gorgeous this time of year. At the beginning of the walkway there were beautiful climbing purple and blue hydrangeas that reached the top. I stood in the walkway for a second to take it all, then I spun around and clapped with excitement. *This* would be the perfect spot for an engagement photo shoot! Yes, it was settled; Eric and I would hire a photographer and have our engagement shoot on the catwalk surrounded by the beautiful hydrangeas. I was confident I could solve a murder *and* plan a wedding.

Next stop: The Pinecone Bakery. I took a deep breath, and tried to focus more on our engagement photo shoot and less on the cars below. When I'd made it all the way across the catwalk and through the bakery doors, it was well worth the jittery nerves.

Inside, it smelled like fresh and yeasty with lots of sugary icing. Behind the display case, there were dozens of cupcakes—an assortment of red velvet, vanilla, cookies and cream, and rows of cookies. There were chocolate chip, peanut butter oatmeal, and oversized cookies. I ordered two cookies; I was sure Eric would be by the Parkstone later to investigate. His favorite was peanut butter, and I got oatmeal for myself.

"Where have you been?" Mike, the pastry chef, asked. "It's been a while since we've seen you."

"I've been busy planning my wedding," I said, not a complete lie. "And things have been busy at the Parkstone."

His expression looked grave. "We heard about the murder. Mrs. Olive was a loyal customer."

I nodded. He handed me the bag of cookies. Now was the time to investigate. "Do you happen to know if she had any enemies?" It was a longshot, but I thought it was worth it. "At the bake shop?"

"Not here," he said. "We all loved Mrs. Olive." He paused and leaned forward on the register. "But there was one time, a few days ago, when I witnessed a less than pleasant conversation, here in the shop, between her and Mrs—" He shook his head. "I can't remember her name…" He thought about it some more. "She just moved in."

"Mrs. Berry?" I said.

"Yes!" he said. "That's it." He paused. "Cassie, you're a good sleuth. You solved the other murders at the Parkstone, didn't you?"

I blushed, turning the color of the pink icing on the red velvet cupcakes. "Guilty as charged," I said, smiling.

"Well, if you solve this case, come back in and we'll give you a dozen free cupcakes of your choice," he said. "Anything we can do to help solve Mrs. Olive's murder."

I smiled and said goodbye, inching across the catwalk with the gorgeous hydrangeas, and my two cookies. The morning was starting out perfectly, and I thought—besides the murder—there wasn't much else wrong at the Parkstone. Then all of a sudden I smelled smoke.

I ran up the catwalk, forgetting about the great heights and the cars whizzing by below. The burning and smoke smell got stronger the closer I got to the Parkstone. From the foot of the courtyard I could see smoke billowing out of the club room windows in large dark plumes.

Oh no! The Parkstone was on fire! I dropped the cookie bag into the pocket of my magenta frayed A-line dress with capped sleeves, and I took off in my peep-toed shoes. I had to get there quickly. I ran in through the lobby and down the hallway toward the club room. The plumes of smoke got thicker and I began coughing. I put my hand over my face, but couldn't get any closer to the club room. The smoke was just too thick.

I grabbed the fire extinguisher from the hallway wall and closing my eyes and holding my breath, I ran through the club room to put the fire out. I sprayed the extinguisher, but the smoke kept billowing too fast, too thick and too unrelenting.

I retreated down the hallway, covering my face with my arm and called Eric once I was outside on the front lawn. Then I put down the fire extinguisher down and ushered residents out to the front lawn where they'd begun to gather. An ambulance and the fire fighters were at the Parkstone were there in minutes. I stood out on the front lawn trying to see what was going on in the building as the firefighters ushered out more residents, and the ambulance first responders helped those who were having problems breathing from the smoke.

About thirty minutes later, Eric came out of the burning building, and he and the first responders sat me down on the steps on the Parkstone's front lawn hill. Eric sat next to me.

"You should have called me right away," he said. "You're lucky you didn't suffer from minor burns or smoke inhalation."

"But the Parkstone!" I said frantically. "It was burning down!" I looked at my magenta dress that now had smoke soot all over it. "I had to do something." I also hadn't realized how much the fire was blazing until I'd tried to walk into the club room, but the flames had been too fierce. "How is it?" I asked. "Is the *Howl* painting okay?"

"The painting is fine," he said. "That was on the wall that the fire didn't get to, but there's something else. And I don't know if now is a good time for you to find out."

What else could there be? First there was a murder, now the Parkstone nearly burned down. What next? Just then, Detective Williams walked through the front door and onto the lawn and said, "Cassie, since when did you have an enemy?"

Eric frowned. He glared at Detective Williams and said, "We were trying not to tell her."

"Tell me what?" I said, putting my heel down.

Detective Williams stepped to the side. "Maybe you should see for yourself."

I was wrapped up in a blanket given to me by the first responders, and I didn't feel like moving from the step I'd been sitting on, but I needed to know what Detective Williams was talking about. Eric held my hand as we walked down the hallways, which were charred. We reached the club room and from the doorway, I could see letters written on the wall: *Back off, Cassie.*

I gasped! Who would do this? How could someone be so cruel as to destroy property *and* write a threat.

Eric squeezed my hand. "Any idea who this could be from?"

"No," I said, "none at all. If anything, I've just been showing understanding to residents during this time of unease after the murder."

Eric shook his head. "Well, there's someone who thinks otherwise, and they're not afraid to destroy property to prove it."

"As long as the *Howl* painting is okay," I said, looking at the painting hanging on the far wall. It was worth millions, and Royce would have been quite unhappy if it had gone up in flames. "I know it means a great deal to Royce."

The painting was safe, but the damage had been done. And there was a lot of it. The fire had torn through one wall in the club room, now exposing the rundown cigar lounge, which was a hidden room on the other side. I'd have to write a note to Royce informing him of the fire and describing the damage. I reached into my pocket and brought out the cookies that I'd dropped on the grass during my fright earlier when the Parkstone was burning in flames. The cookies were still safe. I handed Eric the peanut butter one and I gingerly took out my oatmeal cookie, as if somebody was watching my every move. Then I took a large bite out of the cookie. Something had to go right this morning.

*****

Eric stuck around investigating the fire as I went back to the concierge desk to write a letter to Royce. It had been a little more than an hour since the fire had been put out and the lobby still smelled of smoke.

As always, Jet-Setter and Cashmere wanted attention, and thankfully they'd been in the courtyard when the fire happened. They jumped on the desk and curled up next to me as I typed.

Dear Royce,

There is bad news to report. There has been a fire at Parkstone. No one was injured, thankfully, but there is severe damage to the club room and cigar lounge. So far, no suspects in the arson, but the detectives are investigating the scene as I type.

I will write again when there is an update. For now, know that things are as good as they can be.

Cassie Hall

Eric rounded the corner from the hallway and approached the concierge desk. "Cassie, do you believe me now?"

"About what?" I said.

He put his hands on my shoulders. "That sleuthing is dangerous."

I nodded. "I'm a little more convinced now, yes."

"Great," he said.

"But I'd be lying if I said that was going to stop me from sleuthing."

He looked discouraged. "Do you know of anyone who is out to get you?"

"No," I said. "I'm a great concierge, and I don't know anyone who would say otherwise." Then I thought back to my conversation with my mom the night before, about the information she'd given me about the fire on the set of *Rocky Lakes* many years ago. Coincidence? Or did these two fires have a connection?

I told Eric what I knew about the on-set fire during the filming of *Rocky Lakes*, but he didn't seem to think there was a connection. He said, "That would be implying that someone knew who Dot Olive was, and that Dot lived here, and that person lived here, too."

I knew it was a longshot. "If someone is out to get me, they could have been equally bent on killing Mrs. Olive."

Eric nodded. "Good point. But who could it be? How can we discover who moved to this building because of Dot?"

I thought about it a second. "Here's a rundown of recent move-ins: the Berrys and the Rhodes and Mr. Eager with his two lovebirds," I said.

"And out of those, do any of them have a connection to Dot, *Rocky Lakes*, or Colorado?"

I shook my head. "Not that I know of," I said. Then I thought about it some more, and said, "but Mrs. Penelope Rhodes acts in commercials. She was practicing her lines for that paper towel ad the other day when I was in her apartment."

"Cassie, you're brilliant," he said. "Every time I think it's too dangerous for you to sleuth, you come up with an amazing slant to the case."

"Is there a way we can tell if I'm right?" I said, thinking we still needed more evidence to pin down the culprit.

"I'll interview all the couples again," he said. "Detective Williams and I, that is, and I'll let you know what we find."

For once, I was okay with letting Eric and Detective Williams do the legwork. I didn't want to aggravate the culprit any more than I'd already done unknowingly. *Plus*, I thought, *if I lay low, the culprit won't know my next move.*

Then I remembered something I wanted to tell my detective fiancé. "Eric," I said, before he turned to walk away. "I found the perfect place for us to take our engagement photos: the catwalk in the courtyard. It's surrounded by hydrangeas and will be beautiful in spring."

He smiled and nodded. "Check it off our wedding list."

I kicked up my heels. Perfect.

*****

As far as the arson incident was concerned, resident inquiries about the fire were fierce: When did it start? Was it arson? And will there be another? I answered the questions the best I could without giving away the fact that I thought it was arson. Instead, I said the blaze was likely due to wood leftover in the club room's fireplace. It was believable that because of the hot temperatures outside, a spark could have ignited a flame. There was no need to worry the residents if I didn't have to.

Then, as if rumors that ran quicker than wildfires weren't enough, the local news station set up camp on the manicured front lawn of the Parkstone. From the front lobby windows, I could see reporters interviewing the firemen and detectives on the scene. Mrs. Canterbury and other residents had already gathered in the lobby and were trying to look down the hallway to see the damage. I'd hoped that no one had seen the words *"Back Off, Cassie"* on what was left of the wall between the club room and the cigar lounge. I ushered the residents out to the front lawn. As I made my way back into the Parkstone, I heard a fax come in from Royce. Jet-Setter and Cashmere curled up on the concierge desk as I read what he wrote:

> Dear Cassie,
> I am so sorry to hear the bad news. This is beyond comprehension and it pains me to think I cannot make sense of events at the Parkstone as of late. The only solace is that you and the other Parkstone residents were not harmed by such a malicious act. I will reach out shortly in regards to the future of the club room and cigar lounge.
> Royce Baxter,
> Baxter Enterprises

Out of the corner of my eye, I saw Mrs. Berry, and I remembered what Mike the pastry chef had said about the disagreement between her and Mrs. Olive.

"Mrs. Berry," I said, catching her off guard. "I imagine the move in to the Parkstone has been somewhat jarring," I said, wishing she and Mr. Berry had picked a better week to move in.

Her gaze was not on me, but down the hallway. The fire had captured everyone's interest, and I was hoping the caution tape around the room would deter lookey loos. "This is horrible," she said. "Fires are my worst nightmare. Thank goodness no one was hurt."

Then I thought I'd just cut to the chase. "Again, if you have any information as to who could have killed Mrs. Olive, or set the fires, let me or the detectives know." I paused. "It's funny how you didn't tell me that you fought with Mrs. Olive at the bakery just days ago."

Then Mrs. Berry turned a shade of red. "How do you know about that?"

Now all her attention was on me. Had I found a lead on the case? "How don't I?" I said. "All the pastry chefs were talking about it when I walked into Pinecone Bakery the other day." This was a bit of a fib.

I didn't know she lived at the Parkstone at the time," she said, meeting my eyes. "Although I should have assumed. It was actually before I saw her at swim club. And it wasn't a major disagreement. I was there to pick up a cake for Mr. Berry to commemorate our move-in day, and Mrs. Olive blatantly cut in the line."

My heart dropped. "That's all?" I said, disappointed that the encounter most likely had nothing to do with the case. "And then you were upset?"

She hesitated. "Well, not quite," she said. I looked at her intently as she continued, "I brought it to her attention that she'd skipped the line, and then she said she had a very important cake to get for a Mr. Gillrot. I know his name because it was spelled out in icing on the cake." Mrs. Berry looked very pleased with herself that she'd figured out that mystery, and the thought crossed my mind that I was not the only sleuth at Parkstone. She took a deep breath and continued, "Apparently it was her friend, Mr. Gillrot's, birthday. And then she asked a zillion questions about everything behind the case while her cake was being made, and the rest of us had to wait in line." She tossed her arms up in the air as if to give up. "I mean, what were we supposed to do?"

Mr. Gillrot! I knew he knew more about Mrs. Olive than he was letting on. *He was friends with her,* I thought. *Such good friends that she bought the ornery resident a birthday cake!*

Mrs. Berry continued. "So when she finally got the cake and was walking past me out the door, I kicked my leg out in frustration, and, well, it accidentally hit her shin and the cake toppled on top of her." She paused with an ever so slight smirk. "*Then* she was quite upset."

"She got another cake made—for free—and I picked out a very nice cherry chocolate cake for Mr. Berry and me. So it all worked out in the end." Then she appeared to think about it some more. "Although it *was* slightly awkward when I saw her at swim club a couple of hours later."

"I can imagine," I said, wondering how much went on between the Parkstone residents that I didn't know about. I'm guessing it was a lot. I thought back and remembered the awkward reactions between Mrs. Berry and Mrs. Olive when they saw each other at the pool that first morning of swim club. That explained it.

Following this new lead from Mrs. Berry, I was hot on the trail in a new direction.

My next move would be to investigate Mr. Gillrot's involvement. I thanked Mrs. Berry and asked her to wait outside until the firefighters informed us it was safe to be in the Parkstone again. Except, of course, for the murderer on the loose.

Then I spotted Mr. Gillrot in the crowd on the Parkstone lawn; he was always the tallest resident, so easy to spot.

Mr. Gillrot also usually had his arms crossed and looked defiant. He was also usually wearing a plaid button down shirt, jeans and sandals. Today was no different.

"Do you have a minute?" I said as he towered over me.

"Only if it's not about the murder," he said.

I smiled. "It's not. It's about cake."

His face dropped and his eyes looked discerning. "What about cake?"

I knew I was onto something. "A certain birthday cake from Pinecone Bakery," I said. "And you were the recipient."

"How do you know about that?" he said looking incredulous.

I winked. "I've got my sources."

"All right, Mrs. Know-It-All concierge, what do you want to know that you don't already?" he said. His face look heated. I'd already tried to put out one fire today; I wasn't looking to start another. But here was Mr. Gillrot standing in front of me, fuming.

"How well did you know Mrs. Olive?" I said.

"Dot?" he said.

"Yes," I said, as if there were more than one Mrs. Olive at Parkstone.

He thought about it and said, "Pretty well. But not until well after she was already famous."

I lowered my voice and leaned in closer. "So you know our very own Dot Olive was a famous leading lady?"

"Of course," he said. "*Rocky Lakes*. I used to watch the movie all the time. Maybe not a lot of people knew she was a movie star, but I did. And I didn't dislike her, which for me is saying a lot. She was always so generous and she brought me a cake for my birthday. Not a lot of people knew it was my birthday four days ago. So I guess we all have our secrets."

I smiled. I didn't think there was anything to suspect between Mr. Gillrot and Mrs. Olive, but I had one more question to ask. "Do you know of any other residents who knew she was a celebrity?"

"I guarantee you most people don't know," he said. "*Rocky Lakes* had a cult following, and it was popular, but about thirty years ago. I don't know too many people who would recognize her today."

"Mr. Gillrot, you've been very helpful," I said, "and happy belated birthday."

He shook his hands in the air. "Exactly what I was trying to avoid!"

Chapter 8

After hours had passed, the fire department cleared the Parkstone for residents to reenter. Most residents, after they came back in from the front lawn, decided to mill around the lobby and look at the damage from behind the yellow caution tape. I could hear the phone ringing over their murmurs. I picked it up on the last ring. It was Royce!

"Cassie, is everyone all right?" he said. "I called earlier and no one answered. I was afraid the whole place had burned down." He sounded very alarmed, and I'd hated to bother him during his busy day, but this was an emergency.

"After the fire we were asked to stay outside on the front lawn. Everyone's fine, but the wall between the club room and the cigar lounge isn't," I said. "It's very, very burnt. And the cigar room floor is in shambles."

I expected the tone of his voice to get even graver, but instead he said, "Don't worry about that. We were going to renovate the cigar lounge and turn it into a parlor anyway. That was going to be a future endeavor, which will now become near future." He paused. "As in, I guess, the process has already started."

"A parlor?" I said, noting it was the first I was hearing of it.

"Yes, where residents can sit and read, play games and prattle on about their day. Kind of like the club room, but a bit fancier," he said. "Think of it as a place for comfort and magnificence."

I thought about the charred wall. There was a long way to go to make the parlor idea come to fruition. "Well, I guess if that was the plan all along, the damage is not as devastating, but there's still an arsonist loose in the building, along with a killer," I said, scrutinizing each resident as they walked past the concierge desk. *I wonder if Ginnie Langford set things aflame? Or did Mr. Berry use his cigar lighter to enflame the club room wall?* My mind wondered. "We're close to catching the killer, and this just makes the desire to more immediate."

"We?" Royce said. "I was hoping you'd leave the detective work up to the detectives. There are enough concierge duties to keep you busy. And before I forget, corporate will be sending cupcakes and more truffles to the Parkstone today, to take residents' minds off the fire. Is there anything else you need?"

A place to work that wasn't so chaotic? I shook away that thought. Nothing could make me want to leave the Parkstone, not even graffiti that read: "*Back off, Cassie!*" on a scorched wall. I wasn't going to let up on my end of the investigation. And I wouldn't let Royce down. I assured him we were living luxuriously at the Parkstone, despite the fire, and the sooner the construction crew could renovate the parlor, the better. Another amenity for residents to enjoy would be magnificent.

As I hung up the phone with Royce, Mr. Rhodes approached the concierge desk and said, "My t-shirt. What do you think? Is it working or not?"

I was sure he was going to have a comment about the fire, the damage, the fact we had to stay outside for a couple of hours in the sweltering humidity, or something along those lines. But, his t-shirt? It looked like a perfectly fine cotton shirt to me. "Burgundy is a great color," I said, admiring his outfit.

He shook his head. "Not me, Cassie," he said, looking down at his Chihuahua. "Moola."

I looked down and noticed that Moola was wearing a light blue t-shirt. Mr. Rhodes continued, "She's a contestant in Bethesda's Annual Dog Show next weekend. Remember, Cassie? We've only been talking about it for months."

The Annual Dog Show. Yes. I'd forgotten. It was going to be held in front of the Parkstone, on the main street, Ivy Terrace. Oh, how I hoped we'd find the killer by then. It was going to be a chaotic scene. I remembered the festival from last year. There was music, and dogs walking around on the main stage which was set up in the middle of the street. On top of that, there were dogs sitting on the Parkstone lawn and yapping at residents as they walked in and out of the lobby's revolving doors. I was really looking forward to a vacation with Eric in a little more than a week. Bethesda's Annual Dog Show was the last thing on my mind.

"What do you think about her walk?" Mr. Rhodes said, as he guided Moola down the hall and back.

I was speechless. I didn't really understand the demands of the Annual Dog Show, but thought it was great that Mr. Rhodes was taking it so seriously. "She's going to be great at the show," I said.

I looked down at my magenta colored dress that was still covered in soot. I'd need to go upstairs and change, but right then, his wife, Mrs. Penelope Rhodes, came walking straight through the lobby's doors right toward us. She turned to Mr. Rhodes, kissed him, and then handed him a bag of groceries. "I remembered the kale," she said, before turning to me. "And, Cassie, why do you look so glum?"

There were so many ways to answer that question: my dress was a mess, I'd been threatened by a killer, and there had just been a major fire on the Parkstone property. "I'm just happy the damage wasn't worse," I said, finally.

"What could be worse than that?" she said. "Just like in my paper towel commercial for Spark Clean." Then she put on a fake grin and her actress voice: "Because picking up a spill shouldn't be a pill." She paused. Mr. Rhodes started clapping, which seemed to make Mrs. Rhodes overjoyed. She continued, "I like your attitude of pick up the mess and move on. And my guess is you'll stop sleuthing, right?"

Mr. Rhodes seemed to perk up at this question, as well. Even Moola's ears leaned forward.

"I'm so far from this case, you'd have to use a telescope from the observatory to find me near it," I said, which was only halfway true.

She smiled. "Cassie, I think that's best for everyone."

Why did she care if I was off the case or not? Unless she had something to hide. I had to find out if there was a connection between Mrs. Penelope Rhodes and Mrs. Dot Olive. The only thing I could think of now was that they were both actresses. But Mrs. Rhodes wasn't in *Rocky Lakes*, so they couldn't have known each other from that movie. She and Mr. Rhodes were from Los Angeles, California, and as far as I knew, they'd never lived in the Midwest. I just didn't see how their lives would have every crossed with Dot Olive's.

I watched them walk away, as Mrs. Rhodes turned around with a smirk on her face. Why did she look so mischievous? I had a hunch there might be another fire to put out.

*****

After my shift ended, I decided to go straight back to my apartment. My mom, Eleanor Hall, would be arriving soon, and what a chaotic day for her to arrive.

As a nurse, she was very organized, and she already had our itinerary planned. There were two estate sales in Washington D.C., three neighborhood second-hand shops, and one wedding dress shop in Bethesda we had planned to visit in the next few days. I was already nervous about finding the perfect dress, and now things at the Parkstone were a mess. I tried to tell myself not to let the fire and the murder weigh me down while I was trying on dresses. And I was happy my mom was able to fly in for the occasion. Then she'd be happy knowing I'd found the perfect wedding dress, and it was one more thing I could cross off my wedding list.

I quickly cleaned up my apartment for her visit, which I knew wouldn't seem like long enough. Sometimes I thought I'd move back to Cherry Creek, Colorado, but the hit-and-run death of my high school friend Hunter Appleby had tarnished my perspective on the small town. Everywhere I shopped, ate, and strolled reminded me of him. And for now, as crazy as it was, the Parkstone was a good place to live. There were interesting residents, cupcakes and sweets at the ready, catered Sunday brunches, a swimming pool (when it wasn't a crime scene) and a gorgeous courtyard. As much as my mom would remind me of home, I think I'd made a good move following Eric to Bethesda, MD.

I finished cleaning up my apartment with thoughts of what my wedding dress might look like. Now when I used Spark Clean paper towels it reminded me of Mrs. Rhodes' commercial: "Because picking up a spill shouldn't be a pill." There was something very suspicious about that woman. Moments later, I got a text message from my mom. She was in the lobby. I couldn't wait to see her.

I ran downstairs to see her seated on one of the velvet plush chairs next to Mr. Gillrot—of all residents! I would need to save her from his disgruntled demeanor. She looked very stylish in a bright orange jacket with straight leg black jeans and a bright green scarf tied with a perfect square knot. And what was surprising is that she didn't seem at all phased by Mr. Gillrot's company. "What's that smoke smell, Cassie?" she said, covering her mouth and nose.

"There was a fire in the club room, but it's extinguished," I said, discouraged that the smoke smell was still around. This was my mom's first visit to the Parkstone, and the Parkstone wasn't making a good first impression.

She looked bewildered. "Was it intentional?"

"The detectives are still looking into it," I said, believing the fire was the work of an arson.

"Detectives? So Eric is here?"

I nodded. She continued, "If so, I'd love to talk with him about how this place isn't safe. Maybe there could be a security guard who could keep watch 24/7."

"Mom!" I said. The Parkstone troubles were the last things I needed to add to the stress of wedding dress shopping.

Mr. Gillrot gave a cheer. "That's what I've been saying all along. I want a security guard presence here day and night, and a discounted rate each month—pro-rated for each murder."

She nodded. "It's just dreadful—murders, now fires," she said.

I'd never seen Mr. Gillrot so agreeable. Then he said, "Cassie, your mom is right. You should listen to her more often."

"Royce makes the decisions about rent, Mr. Gillrot," I said. "You know that. And there's no reason to talk poorly about the Parkstone. It's a great place to live."

Then Mr. Gillrot said, "I would point out the irony of that sentence."

My mother laughed. They got a kick out of each other. I hadn't expected to contend with this.

I didn't think it was a good idea for my mom to be colluding with Mr. Gillrot, of all residents. They seemed to be enjoying themselves, but I didn't want his ornery personality to become a problem. I knew Mr. Gillrot's mood would inevitably turn sour.

We said goodbye to him and I showed my mom to her guest room. The only one left was the one where Mrs. Dot Olive had been staying when her plumbing leak caused her to leave her apartment for a night.

Mom settled in and unpacked her bags, meticulously hanging her fashionable clothes in the armoire and gave me a rundown of the new items she'd bought. "Approve?" she said. "You're the one with a good eye for fashion."

She had a knack for piecing together the most stylish outfits. It's where I got my killer fashion sense!

Then she stared at the antique white armoire. She also had a knack for furniture and interior design. "I don't think this should be so close to the door," she said, shaking her head. "What do you think, Cassie?"

She asked what I thought, but I knew if she thought it was too close to the door then that's the answer she was looking for. "It didn't cross my mind," I said. "I'm in charge of booking these rooms for residents and their guests. I've never given any thought to re-designing them."

"It's just that I think the armoire could be more in the center," she said. She began to push the armoire along the wall toward the middle of the room. She's a slender woman, and I got on the other side to help pull the armoire away from the door.

Suddenly, my mom gasped. "Why, what's this? There's a note!"

I ran around the side of the armoire and followed her gaze. There was a folded note on the floor. I motioned her to pick it up, but she'd already bent down to get it. Her face turned pale as she began to read the words.

I got nervous. Had she stumbled across a clue in the mystery? I hadn't thought to search Mrs. Olive's *guest* room for clues. *Why hadn't I thought of that?* My mom put her hand to her cheek in disbelief and then said, "Dear, does this make sense to you?"

She handed me the note. In perfectly cursive handwriting the note read: *"Didn't get what you want?"*

I gasped! How horrible. This must be a letter from the killer. I remembered the night I'd come up to the guest room to check on Mrs. Olive and she'd seemed really frazzled and paranoid. Had someone thwarted something Mrs. Olive wanted? What didn't she get?

As I was caught up with thoughts of the murder, I saw my mom survey the armoire. "Come to think of it, maybe it was better off to the side a bit?" she said.

I turned to my mom, who probably had no interest in sleuthing. "I can't believe we found this note. Of all the weeks for you to visit Parkstone, this is a crazy one."

She gripped my arm. "Do you think we're in danger?"

I shook my head. "Not now," I said. "But I think Mrs. Olive was. And this note proves the murder was most likely premeditated."

"You're speaking like a true detective, like on the sleuth shows I watch," she said. "In a way, it's fascinating, Cassie, that we found the clue, and under the armoire no less. But I wouldn't make a habit of chasing a murderer around the Parkstone. It could lead to trouble. For your own safety, let Eric and the real detectives investigate. All right?"

I'd solved the last three murders at the Parkstone, so the last thing I was going to do was stay away, but I wanted to loop Eric in on the latest clue.

"I'm going to call Eric now," I said, knowing he'd be thrilled at the find.

"And postpone your dress shopping?" she said.

"Yes," I said. "Do you mind?"

She shook her head. "We'll find you the perfect dress," she said, "whenever we shop. And I'd love to check out the courtyard."

"Great idea!" I said, hoping we wouldn't run into Mr. Gillrot again. The courtyard was a mellow place where I was sure there'd be no chaos. "Let's go there now." The mystery of finding the perfect wedding dress would start tomorrow.

*****

The next day found Mom and me at the wedding shop. It was cozy and serene. There was a flurry of wedding dresses as I tried on and showcased different examples in front of the three-way mirror, as my mom interjected her criticisms and affirmations.

The one I had on now I was sure was a no-go. It was too frumpy.

"That has too many ruffles," I could hear my mom's voice say even before I'd made it out of the dressing room of the small shop.

"I like the ruffles," I said.

"Maybe one or two on the sleeves, but not an entire dress of them," she said. "It's supposed to be an elegant wedding dress."

My mom, I was learning, had very strong opinions on wedding dresses. Strong opinions—maybe she and Mr. Gillrot had more in common than I'd originally thought.

The shop was busy and I'd already tried on seven dresses, with five more left to go. *Deep breath.* And with each dress, my mom found something more and more menacing. First, it was too many ruffles, and the next dress, the sleeves were too poofy, and the next had too many beads, and the last had too many layers and so on. I left the shop exhausted from the all of the failed possibilities.

Then we headed to a second-hand shop in Bethesda that had a couple of dresses that both my mom and I agreed looked too old-fashioned. Then we drove to an estate sale my mom had found out about on Foxboro Road in North West Washington, D.C. It was worth a try, but after the last dress shop, I was beginning to think I'd rather be with Eric and the other detectives tracking down a killer rather than wedding dress shopping.

We pulled up to the house, which was expansive. Even from the edge of the front lawn, it was a trek just to reach the house. There were home items like mirrors, records, stereos, books, and paintings strewn about the lawn.

Inside there was a gorgeous grand piano, more paintings, and expensive Villeroy and Boch dinner sets and fancy silver serving trays. My mom loved Villeroy and Boch, and I had a hunch whether or not I found a dress, she'd probably find a new accessory for her kitchen.

We walked into the den area, and my mom spotted a wedding dress hanging from the closet door, next to an old wooden writing desk.

"This is gorgeous!" she gushed.

The dress was beautiful with skinny straps, a heart-shaped neckline and just the right amount of beads on the corset, and it was my size. What were the chances?

"I'm going to try it on," I said, with a smile.

When I took the dress off the hanger, I looked at the tag, realizing it was a Versace. I'd never owned anything by the revered designer, and would love to walk down the aisle wearing his design. I tried the dress on and even my mom agreed it was the perfect dress. It was a bit snug in the waist area, but I'd do sit ups and go for runs—anything to wear this Versace dress.

"I think that's the one," my mom said as I walked around the den swaying in the gown.

"Finally," I said. "It's perfect."

"Are you going to take it?" she said.

I nodded.

"Just make sure Eric doesn't see you in it before the wedding. It's bad luck."

The Parkstone had enough bad luck to go around. And we didn't need more of it. I was certain I could keep Eric from seeing my dress. We didn't live together yet, which in this instance made things easier. But I'd be sure to keep it out of plain sight—away from his sharp detective eye.

Chapter 9

Once we were back at the Parkstone with my wedding dress bag, we retrieved my mom's luggage from the haunted guest room and moved them into my apartment. That way she didn't have to stay in the creepy accommodations, not after finding the threatening note.

My mom unpacked again, and I took my wedding dress and hid it under my bed, where I was sure Eric wouldn't look. I wanted this wedding to be perfect, and that started now. There would be no way Eric would see it before the wedding.

That evening we went back to the courtyard. My mom liked the mix of wrought iron tables and benches, and wicker accent chairs. Then there were my favorite skirted monogrammed camelback chairs, and ornate garden stools near the pond and croquet court.

We took a seat on the wrought iron bench and watched Mr. Berry and Mr. Gillrot try and enjoy a game of croquet without arguing, which was proving to be about as fruitful as me trying to stay away from the murder case. When there was a lull in the action, my mom turned to me and said, "I ran into Hunter's mom the other day."

I could feel that chill run up my arms again. Hunter Appleby was a high school friend who I'd been walking across a crosswalk with one day when he was killed by a hit-and-run driver. The case was unsolved. In the chaos of the accident, I didn't get a license plate number or car model and make. I couldn't help but think that if I had, the murder would have been solved by now. It may have been why I now have such a keen interest in solving crimes. I never want to miss a beat.

My mom continued, "She asked how you were doing."

I gulped. A tinge of guilt swept over me. Hunter had been walking in front. If our positions had been reversed... I guess it just came down to luck. Maybe it explained why I like detective procedurals so much— with all the clues and facts and evidence. I just know that after more than a decade, the only clues that had in Hunter's death were the tire type and the speed range the car was going. I wondered if we'd ever find the killer.

"I'm glad to hear she asked," I said.

"I told her you were doing well."

I smiled, but tried to concentrate on the croquet game, not wanting to talk about the incident anymore. Just then, I heard a male and female arguing. It was coming from above.

My mom looked startled. "What's going on?"

"A couple is arguing," I said. "It sounds like their voices are coming from one of the top floors. I ran out to the middle of the courtyard and looked up. I could see residents on the tenth-floor cacti terrace, engaged in a lively argument.

The male's voice said, "What was I supposed to do?"

"Well, not that!" the woman said.

"Why don't you make all the decisions around here," he said, "then you'll be happy with how everything turns out."

I ran up through the courtyard. "Cassie, come back!" my mom said. "Don't go toward danger."

"I have to see what's going on," I said, rushing out of the courtyard and through the building. I took the elevators to the tenth floor. I flung the terrace doors open to find Mr. And Mrs. Rhodes standing so close together that their foreheads were almost pressed on each other. Moola was curled up at their feet looking up at both of them.

"Is everything all right?" I asked.

Mrs. Rhodes crossed her arms. "Isn't your shift over, Cassie? Why are you snooping around up here?"

"Your yelling was loud, and I wanted to make sure everything was okay," I said.

"I don't buy it," she said. "You're just trying to snoop. And it's not going to work. Let's go, Dash."

Mr. Rhodes picked up Moola, but took his time following Mrs. Rhodes. She scoffed and pulled Moola out of his arms. He lost his balance and braced his fall with one hand which landed on a cactus.

He screamed, and I panicked. Mrs. Rhodes was a brute.

How could she push Mr. Rhodes, into a cactus? Moments later, my mom and Mr. Gillrot appeared in the doorway of the cacti terrace. I was so happy to see them. My mom gasped.

Mr. Gillrot shook his head. "Can we ever get a moment of peace and quiet at the Parkstone?"

My mom grabbed Mr. Rhodes' hand which had been flailing about in pain from the prickles.

Then Mrs. Rhodes piped in, "I'm sorry. Dash. I didn't mean to get mad at you."

Then my mom, who's a nurse, looked at Mr. Rhodes and said, "Hold still." She plucked the cactus prickles from his hand as he said *ouch* with each one. Then she took out a handkerchief and placed it around his hand. "Apply pressure, and you'll be fine in no time. It's probably a good idea to stay away from the cacti."

Mr. Rhodes and Mrs. Rhodes left the terrace.

Mr. Gillrot shook his head. "What's going on in this crazy residence?"

My mom rolled her eyes. "Cassie?"

I shrugged. "Your guess is as good as mine."

I looked at all the cacti surrounding the terrace's walls. I didn't know exactly what the Rhodes were arguing about but it seemed like a prickly situation.

Back at the croquet court, my mom couldn't believe I had chased down those voices and investigated.

"Your job at the Parkstone is as a concierge," she said. "I'm going to worry about you if I think you're sleuthing and investigating every sound you hear in every nook and cranny in this mysterious building."

I assured her I left the sleuthing up to Eric, but that resident disturbances were of my concern.

"I just don't want to see you in a dangerous situation," she said.

Just then we heard a mallet hitting a croquet ball that flew in our direction.

"Narrow misses are everywhere," I said.

"Well, if you aren't going to stop sleuthing the case," she said, "I hope you solve it quickly."

*****

The next morning my mom left Parkstone to go to Reagan International Airport for her 8:00 a.m. flight back to Colorado. She wished me luck solving the case, and said she'd enjoyed her visit. I was glad she'd gotten a break from working at the hospital, and I was grateful she'd cared for Mr. Rhodes when he needed help. I was also happy she'd had purchased a Villeroy and Boch floral cottage teapot from the estate sale to bring home with her. I promised to let her know about any updates in the case as she walked out through the Parkstone revolving doors and said, "Stay out of trouble."

Moments later, Mr. Gillrot appeared in the lobby. Speaking of trouble...The first thing he did was ask about my mom. "It was very nice meeting Eleanor," he said. "Very lovely woman."

I smiled, as I took my post at the concierge desk. The ornery Mr. Gillrot was smitten. "At least she doesn't have too far to travel today. Only halfway across the country." He paused. "Maybe next time she stops by, I'll ask her out to dinner."

Mr. Gillrot seemed much less disgruntled when he was head over heels. "Or out to the theater. Cassie, did you ever get a hold of those tickets?" I was beginning to think he might even be a good person to add to my wedding guest list.

"I think that would be grand," I said.

"Then I shall," he said.

"And about the theater," I said. "The tickets are sold out, but I know one of the ushers who said he thinks he can get me two extras."

"Spectacular!" Then this was one of the rare occasions when Mr. Gillrot smiled. He walked away with his head up high through the courtyard doors. I was flipping through all the maintenance requests for that day: Leaky toilet, broken garbage disposal, bulb needed for light fixture. I'd taken two days off for dress shopping, and I was coming back to a lot of work.

As I sorted through all of the requests, I sensed the presence of someone in front of me. It was Mary Chris Farley. She looked pale and uneasy.

"Cassie, do you have a minute?" she said. "It's about Mrs. Olive's murder."

I always had a minute to devote to the case. I put aside the requests and gave her my full attention.

She looked from side to side as if checking to see if anyone else was around. The she began talking slowly. "I saw Mrs. Olive the morning she was killed," she said. "She stopped by my apartment to recruit me for swim club. She said she'd been up on the rooftop at the pool that morning, and that Mrs. Kemper had stopped by to eat one of the blueberry cupcakes she had made her, and then had left. And Mrs. Olive said that no one else had showed up to swim. I said I'd be right up and that I was planning on going, but I'd slept in." She paused. "I didn't tell you or Eric because I was afraid I'd be implicated somehow, but since the culprit hasn't been nabbed, I thought maybe this information could help."

"Do you remember exactly what she said?" I asked, relieved that we had some more details about the sequence of events from that morning.

"She said Mrs. Kemper had been by to try one of the cupcakes, but other than her, no one was at swim club, and did I plan on heading up to the pool?" She paused. "I said I'd be there as soon as I got ready. Then I took the stairs up to the rooftop, and that's when I saw you, Cassie."

Mary Chris looked genuinely distraught. She was gripping the handles of her purse when she talked, and made quick sideways glances.

I wondered how Mrs. Olive had appeared that morning. "Did she seem frazzled or upset?"

Mary Chris shook her head. "No, just discouraged. She always took swim club so seriously. And even though she was controlling about my back stroke, I wouldn't have wanted anything bad to happen to her."

I nodded. "Of course not." Now the important part would be to piece together the timeline of events after Mrs. Olive left Mary Chris' apartment. What else had transpired at the pool? And what had caused her to hit her head and die?

"I'll be sure to let Eric know about this recent development," I said. "I think it could be helpful in solving the case."

Mary Chris smiled. "I hope so. Thanks, Cassie. I feel so much better getting it off my chest."

After she walked to the elevators, I went back to sorting the requests. There was a backlight broken on the lobby level button in the main elevator, the coffee machine needed more water, and the Xerox machine in the business room was jammed. There was never a dull moment at the Parkstone.

I walked outside to do the building rounds. I decided to start at the courtyard. It looked beautiful. The spiral tree topiaries looked grand, and the birds were chirping. I walked along the path next to the observatory and saw resident Ben Harrison, who was finishing up filmmaking classes at George Mason University, in the observatory. Ben's love of the observatory came in handy whenever a resident was accidently locked out on their balcony. Ben was usually the first one to see them waving for help through the observatory telescope.

I slipped into the observatory which was old and creaky. "Any signs of life on the moon?" I said.

"Trying to find Venus, actually," Ben said, looking away from the telescope. "Although, I did spot a faint outline of the moon earlier." Then he peered back through the brass telescope. "Did you know you can see Venus during the daytime? A white speck in the sky—difficult to see now. I'm thinking about making a documentary movie about my quest to find all of the planets."

The observatory was snug, but perfect for residents who wanted to enjoy the night or daytime sky from the comfort of the courtyard.

There were two observatory benches along one side, and a bookshelf with books about the galaxies and backyard observatories along the others.

And in the middle, there was a large brass telescope on a mahogany wood tripod.

I took a seat on the end of the far bench and decided to cut to the chase.

"I noticed you can see the rooftop pool through the telescope," I said. "Any chance you were zoomed in on the rooftop pool area the morning Mrs. Olive was killed?"

He backed away from the telescope and sat down on the bench next to me. "Cassie, I take it you're sleuthing this case, too?"

"I can't help it," I said. "I want to solve the case for Mrs. Olive."

He nodded. "It's like you're drawn to these mysteries like the Earth pulls the moon."

That seemed like a strong analogy but wasn't far off. "Precisely" I said.

"I didn't mention this to the detectives, but I'll tell you, Cassie," he said. "I don't know how important it is. I was here the morning of her murder, and I was preparing to search for Venus, and the telescope was focused on the rooftop. I moved it over slightly and saw Mrs. Olive and Mr. Eager talking and gesturing wildly. Mrs. Olive was gesturing a lot with her hands, and Mr. Eager seemed unconvinced with whatever it was she was saying. But then they moved and weren't within the telescope's line of sight. And I was more interested in the sky anyway. So, if something happened, it was out of my range of sight."

"Thanks, Ben," I said, wishing he'd seen more. But it was strange Mr. Eager had been seen with Mrs. Olive on the rooftop that morning in the first place, because he'd said he was at the pool that morning, and that he left because nobody was there. Why would he lie about that unless he was hiding something?

I'd investigate.

*****

Back at the concierge desk, Lillian, our leasing agent, told me that new residents, the Hadwins, would be stopping by sometime this afternoon to sign their lease. Summer was a busy time in the leasing office, and Lillian seemed stressed. "I hope everything at the Parkstone is under control," she said, leaning across the desk and narrowing her eyes.

"Everything today has been under control, although I'd avoid showing them the fire damaged club room."

"It's just that you're always investigating the case, Cassie, and I want to make sure that you're not going to be confronting residents or something absurd like that when Mr. and Mrs. Hadwin show up. They're very important soon-to-be Parkstonians."

"Got it," I said. "Everything is under control."

She smiled. "Great. I'm glad we're in agreement about that."

After she retreated back to her office, Mr. Beasley came up to the desk to pick up a package.

He signed the digital signature pad, as I brought a large box on a dollie around the concierge desk.

"Thank you, Cassie," he said. "You're always so efficient." He paused. "Did I tell you I'm learning to juggle?"

"You always have a magic trick up your sleeve," I said, "but I didn't know you'd added juggling to your repertoire."

He picked up a pen, the concierge bell and said, "I need one more item."

I walked behind the desk where I found a half empty plastic Sprite bottle. "Will this do?"

"Perfect," he said, and he started juggling them. I was impressed. Then he dropped the Sprite bottle, and the pen dropped, but he was able to catch the bell.

"How did you learn to juggle?" I said.

"I'm taking a break from magic tricks, but still have some work to do," he said, blushing.

He pushed the dollie toward the elevator and I thought about the different suspects Eric and I were juggling in the case, and the differing timeframes of when residents were at the pool. And what if the murderer had been juggling a lot, too? It seemed as though there could have been a lot going on during the murder. It was not an easy open and closed case that just involved someone pushing someone into the cabana.

And whoever did it must have acted quickly!

Chapter 10

That late afternoon, I heard from my mom that she had arrived safely back in Cherry Creek, Colorado, with her new teapot and lots of happy memories. I wrote back to her letting her know that Mr. Gillrot might be after a date the next time she visited. I thought it was good to give her a warning about that sort of thing, especially with the ornery Mr. Gillrot.

Then I turned my phone off. I had wedding plans to make and I didn't want to be distracted. I wrote out the wedding guest list, even inviting Mr. Gillrot. Maybe he could be my mom's plus one?

Then I decided to try my dress on. It looked fantastic! I managed to zip it all the way up even though it was slightly difficult to breath. I'd need to take it to a tailor to get it let out. I looked at the back in the mirror. It was beautiful with the long flowing train. I'd have to practice walking down the aisle with all the fabric. And the clear bead details were dainty and glorious. I'd found the perfect dress.

Suddenly, I heard knocking on my door. It was loud and immediate. Fearing the worst, I breathed in—as deep as I could in the dress—and looked through the peephole. I didn't see anyone. Had there been another development in the case? I looked through the peephole again, but there was no one. They must be standing to the side of the door. I was about to go look for a possible weapon in my apartment when I heard Eric's voice. "Cassie, open the door! I need to talk to you." Then a pause. "Where are you?"

I panicked. What was wrong? He needed me. Without a second thought, I swung the door open. He gasped. "What are you wearing?"

I was caught red-handed. "My wedding dress," I said as more of a question.

He smiled. "You look beautiful."

I grimaced. He wasn't supposed to see it before the wedding. This was bad luck. I had been so eager to open the door, I'd forgotten I was wearing my dress. *The bad luck at Parkstone continued...*

I smoothed the front of the dress and fluffed the train. "This is it," I said. "*The* dress. The one you weren't supposed to see until the wedding."

"You look gorgeous," he said, smiling.

I wasn't thrilled about it at the moment. I'd gone through great lengths to keep the dress a secret and now he'd seen it any way. "What do you want?" I said, wrapping my arms around my waist. "It sounded so urgent."

"I have a new clue in the case," he said, taking out his notebook. "I tried calling you but it went straight to your voicemail."

"I was trying to get wedding planning done," I said.

"In your dress?"

I blushed. "Come in."

Eric took a seat on the loveseat near the balcony door. I still hadn't stepped out on my balcony, because I hadn't gotten over my fear of heights. But, no matter. Why was Eric here? He gave me a mischievous glance and said, "There's new information about the case, and I wanted to tell you first."

Eric rarely told me case information before anyone else. Naturally, I was suspicious. I poured iced tea into two glasses and put hummus and crackers on an appetizer plate, which I placed on the coffee table across from him. Ready to divulge the case secret, Eric clasped his hands together and said, "Strands of Mrs. Olive's hair had a lot of chlorine, blond hair dye and DNA from someone other than her."

"You don't say?" I said.

"So I'm wondering if the killer pulled her hair and she hit her head on the cement that way."

I reached for hummus and crackers. "Anything is possible with this case," I mused.

He continued, "But that also doesn't make sense, because even though there may have been an altercation involving her hair, it's not consistent with how you found her."

"So what are you saying?"

"I'm saying there's no evidence she was pushed," he said. "While someone who was standing in front of her may have pulled her hair, that's not what caused her to fall."

"So you're saying she could have fallen by accident?"

He took a bite of the chips and hummus. "I know it sounds crazy, but she could have accidentally tripped near the pool and hit her head on the cement."

I shook my head. Mrs. Olive was plump, but she was way too athletic to have *accidentally* fallen on the cement, taking the poolside cabana along with her. I believed there was something more sinister at play.

Eric grimaced. "Cassie, I know I always tell you to stay away from the case, but I could really use your help here."

"First, I think she was murdered," I said, smoothing my wedding dress around my legs and admiring the beautiful beading. "I don't think she fell accidentally."

"Any suspect ideas?" he said.

I told him about how I found out that Mr. Eager had lied about being at the pool alone. And that I thought it was worth questioning him again. Eric nodded and I said, "I just hope this doesn't turn into a cold case like Hunter Appleby's. My mom said she ran into Hunter's mom the other day."

He shook his head. "You're never going to get over it, are you, Cassie?"

"Why should I?" I said, standing up from the arm chair. I opened the blinds and looked out the window at the sun-soaked courtyard. The vibrant crab apple trees were like a cloak over the manicured lawn. Residents' laughter emanated from game on the croquet court.

The distance from the scene below made me dizzy.

Then Eric spoke up. "I'm not saying you should get over it. I'm just saying that you can't spend your whole life wondering what you could have done, or why someone driving 62 miles per hour got away."

Suddenly, my body froze. I felt a lump in my throat. *Sixty-two miles per hour?* That was a strange comment. In the police report the detectives had only listed a speed *range* the car was going. And that range was between sixty and seventy miles per hour. How did Eric know, or why did he assume the car had been traveling at precisely sixty-two miles per hour? How could anyone know exactly how fast a car was traveling unless....

Could he have been in the car? Now, the heights below didn't frighten me nearly as much as the potential truth in front of me. Standing stiff in my wedding dress, and keeping my gaze steady on the courtyard, I said, "How did you know the car was going sixty-two miles per hour?"

If there was one question I ever wanted answered, this was it, and Eric didn't have an answer. Quiet moved in like pieces on a chess board. After some time had passed and he still didn't answer, I craned my neck to look at him. "Eric?"

"Cassie," he said.

"Why won't you answer me?"

"I didn't mean to hurt you."

I gripped the edges of my dress.

"You wanted me to propose for the longest time, and I couldn't commit because I didn't want there to be any secrets between us. But obviously there is one."

I gulped. He continued, "Then I caved and proposed when I feared I'd almost lost you after you solved Mason Day's murder."

"But you had a secret, this entire time?" I faced him completely, wanting to know the truth. My knuckles were pale with tension.

"I should have told you sooner. But I'm sworn to secrecy," he said.

"What about your promise to me?"

"I'm sorry."

There was more silence. I breathed in deep, and clenched my knuckles tighter. I could barely catch my breath, and it wasn't because of the corset. Eric had been lying to me about the crash since we'd been in high school—nearly since the time I'd known him. I wasn't going to let him get away with it.

"No," I said, "now you have to come clean. Who was it?"

"I can't, Cassie. I wish you didn't know I know."

"I'm not backing down," I said, giving him my killer stern look.

With that, he leapt up and ran for the door. I picked up the train of my wedding dress, just as his large shoulders bustled out the doorway. I couldn't let him escape.

I followed him down the snug hallway clutching the train of my dress as I ran. The stairwell door opened with a loud bang and he ducked down the stairwell. I followed, picking up more of my dress's train. "Eric!" I yelled, my voice echoing in the stairwell. Hoping he'd respond, I ran to the banister, and looked down. He looked like an ant on the first floor; he was so far ahead of me. He flung the lobby door open in haste and it banged against the wall. This was my only chance. I flung myself around the railing, and wrapped my legs around the pole as I flew down the banister! I was past one flight of stairs and then the next until I reached the ground level.

Then I opened the door as he was crossing through the lobby. I had caught up to him.

He glanced behind his shoulder and yelled, "Stop chasing me, Cassie!"

We ran through the lobby yelling and I was flailing one arm and holding onto my wedding dress with the other. I looked up to see Lillian, the leasing agent, standing in the lobby greeting the new residents, Mr. and Mrs. Hadwin. *Great, just what I needed.* She scowled as I flew past. Then she banged her high heel on the marble floor and said, "Cassie, remember what I said to you. You're out of control!"

Then Mr. Gillrot, who was seated on one of the lobby's plush velvet chairs, craned his neck to see the commotion and said, "Cassie, is your wedding today? I had no idea."

Once I was on the front lawn hill, I lunged to chase after Eric who was leaping down the front steps of the Parkstone. Then my heel caught the side of my dress and I rolled swiftly down the hill. I finally stopped tumbling, landing on the edge of the street next to Eric's car.

Eric was stern. "Cassie, I'm warning you—stop chasing me!"

I hadn't chased him this far to just to give up. I threw myself on the front of his Volvo as Eric ducked into his car, slamming the door and starting his engine.

"Stop the engine," I yelled.

Then the engine stopped. Eric opened his car door and said, "Cassie, get off my car. Don't you think we've made enough of a scene?"

Yes, running and screaming past Mr. Gillrot and Lillian and the new residents was not how I'd planned on spending my afternoon, but I didn't know Eric was keeping such a dark secret. "I'm not leaving until I know who killed Hunter."

"Then I'll leave," Eric said, sidling toward the open car door.

I felt tears well up as Eric shook his head and said, "I make it decades without spilling who did it...I'm not going to say now."

"You're a detective; *you* more than anyone should know you've got to go to the police," I said. "It's been a cold case for years, but it doesn't have to be."

"Everyone's moved on with their lives," he said, ducking into his car. "Everyone but you."

I decided to make a bold decision. I took off my engagement ring and said, "If you don't tell the police who did it, I will *not* marry you." I thought this might convince him to spill the beans.

He watched as I placed my ring on the hood of his car and said, "If you drive away right now, I promise I won't follow you."

But after minutes passed, the thought crossed my mind that he might not follow me either. I gulped. I'd put my foot down. Now it was up to him to decide what he was going to do. I bundled up my dress' train, now with a few light grass stains, and walked up the Parkstone stairs. As I walked through the lobby, Lillian was glaring at me and the Hadwins looked slightly scared.

"I'm sorry for the disturbance," I said.

Lillian just shook her head. "So inconsiderate, Cassie."

Mr. Gillrot walked over to me and said, "Well it's all right. I thought I'd missed your wedding day. Now *that* would be inconsiderate."

I wanted to weep. I'm surer Eric and I had looked crazy just now, like how the Rhodes looked arguing on the cacti terrace the other night. Probably even crazier. And right now I wasn't sure there was going to be a wedding. "You didn't miss it, Mr. Gillrot," I said. "Details are TBD."

"Well, all right," he said. "I hope everything's okay."

Everything was up in the air at this point. There was still no murder suspect in the case of Mrs. Olive, there was a possible suspect in the case of Hunter, and in a matter of minutes, the wedding I'd been planning for months with Eric was doubtful. Only one thing could help. I walked behind the concierge desk, and took a guest gift bag of truffles and ate one as I headed back to my apartment.

*****

The next day at work it was difficult to concentrate––even with a large slice of apricot pie courtesy of Mrs. Canterbury. I sensed that Cashmere and Jet-Setter, who nuzzled his nose into my arm—knew about the fallout between me and Eric and didn't have the same pep. With less than enthusiastic meows, they pawed at the pie plate, but seemed to liven up once I refilled their food bowls.

Between bites of pie, I tended to my duties. I secured the theater tickets for Mr. Gillrot, informed leasing that Mrs. Westlight wanted to break her lease—she'd had enough murders—and the garbage disposal in 210 was causing a leak in 110, which in turn was causing me a headache.

The only thing that seemed vibrant on the concierge desk was the robust bouquet of blue iris and pink tulips with large yellow lilies that had been sent from corporate this week. Each week they sent over a new bouquet and each one was more extravagant than the last. I looked at the huge cement vase. *That could be a weapon*, I thought, *in a lethal potted plot.* Next time there was an irate resident at the concierge desk, I'd keep my eye on the bouquet. Corporate had also sent a box of cupcakes and truffles, which I reminded myself to leave some for the residents, who thankfully seemed to go about business as usual.

Although there was still one person who wasn't too happy with me: Lillian, who went about her day avoiding me. Since the fiasco in front of the Hadwins, she'd given me the cold shoulder, and even a colder stare.

I wondered if I was going to hear from Eric again. Or would my Versace wedding dress continue to hang in the closet? I was the one who'd given him the ultimatum, so it was in his court, and I would go about my day hoping he would make the right choice.

Around 10 a.m.—like Royce instructed—the construction crew showed up to begin renovations on the fire damaged wall and start renovating the cigar lounge into the parlor that Royce envisioned. I walked with them down the hallway, showing them the way to the club room. I opened the club room window to let some fresh air in, and looked at the beautifully manicured hedges. Then my eye caught something plastic and bright on the ground beneath the hedges. It was a bright pink lighter. I climbed out of the window again, snagging my forest green lace top on a sharp wooden splinter in the window pane. I crept onto the hedges and managed to land with both peep-toe shoes on the ground. Then I carefully reached my arm into the hedges until my fingers gripped the lighter. Was this what had been used to start the fire?

How had the fire fighters not spotted it? It was a pink lighter with cupcakes on it. Mrs. Kemper's favorite color was pink, and she liked to bake and eat cupcakes. Could this belong to her? Not necessarily. But did she have a motive? She could also have been set up. I did think Mrs. Rhodes seemed suspicious that day when I saw her after the fire, but didn't have any concrete evidence to prove she was the murderer.

This is something I'd be excited to tell Eric about, but for now I'd keep recording clues on my own. I was running the investigation myself. And tonight there was the perfect opportunity for sleuthing. There was a poolside memorial ceremony for Mrs. Olive, and I'd need all my energy for mingling and questioning. I kept the lighter in my skirt pocket and decided I'd bring it out during the ceremony and gauge residents' reactions to determine who the lighter belonged to.

I walked back to the concierge desk through the courtyard and took away the *"Will be back shortly sign"* just as Mr. Eager approached the desk.

"Cassie," he said, "I've been looking for you."

I placed the lighter on the concierge desk to see if he had any reaction to it, but he didn't, except for a dismayed look that maybe I smoke. "What can I help you with, Mr. Eager?" I still wanted to know why he'd lied about being on the roof deck with Mrs. Olive.

"I would like to rent the club room for a grand chess tournament," he said.

"I'm sorry, Mr. Eager," I said. "But the club room is out of commission until the renovations are made. The workers started today and the renovations should be complete in a month. Then there will be a beautiful parlor for chess games. Also, the pool re-opens this evening."

116 Cabana Corpse

He shook his head. "I don't think I'll be going back to the pool. Probably shouldn't have joined swim club in the first place."

Then I got up enough courage to come right out and ask, "Why didn't you tell me you were at the pool and got into an argument with Mrs. Olive the day she died?"

He took a step back. "I didn't tell you that," he said, "because of how it would make me look. I got into an argument with her the morning she was found dead. That doesn't look good."

I agreed. That put him in the suspect spotlight. "What did you two argue about?"

"She was convinced I should just jump in the pool and get over my fears, and I wanted to take a more, 'walk in the shallow end' approach. Well, when I said I wouldn't just jump in, she crossed her arms, holding her forearms tightly and looking really upset. I know she was the swim club leader, but she didn't have a clue about how to relate to people." He paused. "Then a group of those birds from the ledge swooped down nearly skimming her hair. You know how afraid of birds she was. She kept asking me to check her hair for feathers."

I let out a slight laugh. That could explain why Mr. Eager's DNA had been found on strands of her hair.

He looked startled. "And how did you know I was arguing with her?"

It was thanks to my detective skills, but I figured I'd keep that to myself. "Just a hunch," I said.

"Well, don't go thinking I'm the killer, because I'm not. I left after our argument. I actually fell into the cabana, slightly bending it, on my way out. I was trying to get past Mrs. Olive without falling into the pool. It didn't help that she kept urging me to go in," he said. "I bent the cabana by accident, but that's it. And how you knew I was on the roof deck arguing with her in the first place is a mystery to me."

"I believe you," I said, thinking that would explain the dent in the cabana that Mrs. Berry saw. And Mrs. Olive worrying about the birds was the reason for Mr. Eager checking her hair. Now I just need to figure out how the cabana collapsed completely, with Mrs. Olive dead under it.

Chapter 11

"They'd like to reserve the freight elevator," Lillian said. "And try not to mess up again. Okay, Cassie?"

Things hadn't exactly gone awry. Eric and I just had a disagreement; unfortunately it was in front of residents, co-workers and the two Parkstone fur balls. I would ensure that the Hadwin's move-in would go as planned. I reserved the freight elevator, and handed them two new resident gift bags, complete with topiary-embellished stationary, an engraved pen, and a cupcake from Pinecone Bakery.

Mrs. Hadwin looked thrilled. "Cassie, I think we're just going to love it here." She paused. "And I do hope everything is okay with you since last time we saw you."

I nodded. "More than okay," I said, lying through my teeth. I still hadn't heard from Eric, but that wasn't a reason to worry residents. "If there's anything else I can do to help with your move-in, let me know."

"What do you think, Charles?" Mrs. Hadwin said.

"I love it here already," he said.

They retreated up to the eleventh floor to organize their new place, as the movers brought in their belongings. Everything was quiet at the concierge desk, and I was enjoying this lull in activity. Then I heard my cellphone ring. It was my mom. How would I break it to her that the wedding was off? I answered the call on the last ring.

"Hi, mom," I said hesitantly. "This isn't the best time."

"You won't believe it!" Her voice was shrill. "Good news! The Police have arrested the driver responsible for the hit-and-run that killed Hunter Appleby."

"How?" I said, incredulous.

"The Police have confirmed that after nearly two decades of searching for a suspect in the case, the driver has turned himself in," she said. "Isn't that great? I wish you were here. It's all over the local news."

I let out a huge sigh. "You don't say," I said, wondering about the extent of Eric's involvement in this arrest. "That's the best news I've heard in a long time. So, the case has been solved."

"Well, they haven't released the driver's name yet," she said, "but I've got the TV tuned to the coverage, so I'll let you know as soon as they announce it. I know how this case has affected you even though you don't always admit it. Now you can consider that cold case solved." There was a pause. "Hunter's parents must be so happy."

"What a good surprise," I said, thinking that I'd begun to believe this day would never come. And what a relief. I ate another truffle. I was convinced Eric had somehow done the right thing. He must have convinced whomever the driver was to come clean. Now was he coming back to marry me? I felt my ringless finger.

Before my shift ended, I had to do the building rounds, and I decided to go to the pool to investigate before the ceremony. Jet-Setter and Cashmere followed with me up to the roof deck. The three of us strolled gingerly near the pool. I tried to reenact the series of events that could have taken place the morning of Dot Olive's murder.

With Jet-Setter and Cashmere yapping at my feet, I walked along the poolside cement near the cabana. So, if she wasn't pushed, how did she fall? What if she was running really fast and stumbled? I couldn't seem to think straight.

The heat and humidity of the rooftop encompassed me.

I walked past the pool into the shaded club house, which looked just the same as when the police had left it. I looked to see where Cashmere and Jet-Setter had gone when I heard a scuffling noise in the back corner. I turned and surveyed the club house's nooks and crannies. The noise was coming from underneath a discarded newspaper in the corner. The noise got louder and, before I knew it, an object was coming at me. I ran as it chased me toward the pool: a large, feathery bird skimming above my head as I dove into the deep end.

I stayed under water as long as I could hold my breath, and then popped up for air.

"What was that?" I said out loud. "That bird attacked me!" I caught my breath and swam to the shallow end where I stepped out of the pool. My lace green dress was soaking wet. Cashmere and Jet-Setter had curled up in the chaises and were looking at me befuddled.

It reminded me of the story Mr. Eager had told me about the bird who swooped down into Mrs. Olive's hair.

Suddenly, I heard loud clapping. I looked up to see Eric standing in the roof deck doorway, thoroughly amused. "You're still sleuthing I take it?"

I smiled. "An unexpected underwater investigation."

He laughed, and then became serious. "I wanted you to know the authorities nabbed the hit-and-run driver."

"I heard," I said, ringing the water from my dress. "Means a lot to me." I paused. "I have a hunch you were part of the crime-solving?"

"I've been wanting to tell you the story for so long, and now finally I can tell it to you," he said, looking relieved. He walked down the rooftop steps and sat down on a chaise as I took a seat on the chaise next to him. "That day Robbie Wheeler and I were rushing to see his mom in the hospital."

I gasped. "Robbie Wheeler!" I placed a hand over my mouth. Chills ran up my arms.

"I'm sure you remember his mother in the hospital with abnormal heart tremors. Her condition got worse. She had already had one heart attack and was on the brink of another."

"So you and Robbie were driving to the hospital?"

"We were speeding down Hyacinth Road, trying to get to the hospital as fast as we could." He paused, and tears welled up in his eyes. "Cassie, you were on the other side of the street, about to dart across the crosswalk. I always had a crush on you even back then. Robbie and I were so distracted about getting to the hospital that as we continued down the road, we ignored a loud bang under the car. We didn't realize we'd run over someone until later that night."

I hugged my waist. I shivered in the unrelenting humidity. Eric put his arm around me.

Tears welled in my eyes. "When did you realize it?"

"When I saw you interviewed on the news," he said. "You talked about crossing Hyacinth Road when the accident with Hunter occurred, and as soon as you said it, I remembered seeing you cross the street. I remembered the noise. And this dark suspicion came over me that Robbie had run over Hunter. Robbie checked his tires the next day and found his back tires were dented and the alignment was off. I knew it had been us."

I shook my head. "So why didn't you turn Robbie in?"

"His mom was in such poor condition. And she was like a second mother to me. What would happen if I turned Robbie in?"

And then as if thinking out loud I said, "She would lose her only son."

"She would have no one to take care of her."

It was all making sense now. He continued, "So I've kept my mouth shut all this time. I'm sorry that since we first started dating I've kept this secret from you."

"So how did you convince Robbie to turn himself in?"

"After you and I talked yesterday, I knew it was the right thing to do. I called Robbie. He said his mother had died recently of a heart attack and the guilt from the accident wouldn't go away. He was planning on going to the cops himself anyway." He paused and said, "So I was sort of off the hook."

I laid my head on his shoulder. "Not that any of that was easy."

He placed his hand on my knee. "Cassie," he said and kissed me. Then he looked at my dress and said, "You're dripping wet; how are you going to finish your shift?"

"I'll need to change before going back to the concierge desk," I said, not wanting to go back to work after everything that had happened, but I knew the residents needed me. I looked at my sopping wet dress. "It was worth the investigating." I paused and then said, "I think she was scared. She was running from someone or something and tripped face planted in the cement, taking the cabana with her as she fell."

"That's a great read on the case," he said. "If we find who or what she was running from, we have our culprit."

"Something to that effect," I said, and thought some more about how it could have happened. Maybe it wasn't that simple. "I think we're close." I thought of how scared I was when I'd heard the bird fly out of the club house's shadows. And how much Mrs. Olive feared birds. What if she was being chased by a bird and tripped and fell? What if *no one* was to blame?

As if Eric read my mind he said, "You're thinking maybe it was an accident?"

"I didn't at first, but now it seems possible," I said. Then our eyes met and I said, "But how likely is it that Mrs. Olive took an accidental fatal spill right in front of the cabana?"

"I agree, Cassie. Not likely. We're still searching for a culprit. Plus the fire and the note threatening you to back off screams that it's not an accident."

I nodded. Sometimes it was just good to have confirmation. "Mrs. Olive's memorial ceremony is tonight," I said. "I think you should come."

"I can be there," he said. "Especially now that I'm not keeping any secrets from you."

I began to give him a hug, forgetting that I was sopping wet. He waved me away and said, "I still have to go back to the station after this. I'm just on a late lunch break."

I playfully flicked some water on him with my high heel shoe. "Run while you can."

After Eric left, I gathered the cats, and finished ringing out my sopping wet dress. I carried my heels in my hand and headed to the elevator. My first stop would be back to my apartment to change. Ping! The elevator door opened. I stepped in, only two floors to go. What's the worst that could happen? On the eleventh floor, the elevator door opened. My dress was dripping wet, and the Hadwins were staring back at me quizzically. Mrs. Hadwin turned her head in thought, "Cassie?"

"Hi," I said.

"We were just coming to get you," she said. "And here you are! Great service. We're disagreeing about design elements in the apartment. And I thought maybe you would know best about furniture placement."

With more than two years of experience as the Parkstone's concierge and my mother's keen eye for interior design, I believed I could give it a shot. With my brightest smile and disregarding the fact I was still drenched, I said, "Great!"

*****

That night at the ceremony, I wore a loose black empire waist dress and my second set of peep-toe shoes as the ones I'd worn earlier were still water logged. I also wore my bathing suit underneath so that I could take another bird-free swim in honor of Mrs. Olive after the ceremony.

Many residents showed up to the event. There were the Rhodes,' Mrs. Kemper, Mrs. Canterbury, Mr. Eager, Mr. Gillrot, the Berrys, Ben Harrison and Mary Chris. I was happy with the turn out. Mrs. Canterbury had brought a coconut cake, brownies, and chocolate chip cookies, and I brought lemonade and apple cider.

The humidity was stifling, but that was to be expected in Bethesda, Maryland, in June. The ceremony was somber, and afterwards residents stuck around for conversation and light refreshments. I thought now was a good time to take out the lighter I'd found in the bushes after the fire and see if anyone noticed. I took out the hot pink lighter from my dress and immediately Mrs. Kemper gasped.

"Is this yours?" I asked her, narrowing my eyes.

"Yes, well it *was*," she said. "That's got to be it. Of course, it's mine. How many lighters have cupcakes on it?"

"I found it at the scene of the arson crime," I said. Not so sweet.

Eric gasped. "Cassie," he said, looking me square in the eye. "You found evidence, and you've been keeping it from me? What happened to us not having secrets?"

I was actually so surprised by Eric's visit this afternoon, I'd forgotten to tell him. I looked at the other residents' reactions to the revelation of the lighter. Mrs. Rhodes was the only other one to stand out. Her expression was one of pure smugness.

Mrs. Kemper chimed in. "Where'd you find this, Cassie?" she said.

"In the courtyard," I said, handing her the lighter. "Just stumbled across it, that's all." Mrs. Rhodes' face dropped. *What was she thinking?* I wondered. Was she in disbelief that Eric wasn't apparently going to pursue it as most likely the arsonist's weapon?

"I use it to light the candles on my dining room table," Mrs. Kemper said. "Thanks for finding it."

Mrs. Rhodes tapped her sandaled foot on the ground. "If you found it on the ground, Cassie, don't you think it could have been used by the arson?"

"Yeah, Cassie, where exactly did you find it?" Eric said.

"Near a bench in the courtyard," I said. Now I was beginning to believe that Mrs. Rhodes had found Mrs. Kemper's lighter and had used it to burn down the club room. Just then, I thought about what my mom had said about the fire on the set of *Rocky Lakes*. This might be a stretch, but I thought there might be a connection. I just needed to find the connection between the two fires. And I had a hunch that connection was our resident commercial actress Mrs. Rhodes.

"Gosh, Cassie," Eric said. "I wish you would have told me. I'll need to take that to the station for evidence."

He sealed the lighter in a Ziploc bag and then placed it in his detective briefcase that was resting on a chaise. People began to leave the rooftop one by one and after all of them were gone and it was just me and Eric, I slipped out of my black dress, jumped in the pool, and swam a couple of laps in honor of Mrs. Olive. I heard her voice in my head, giving me pointers on the butterfly stroke. Then Eric dropped his trousers and his shirt, jumped in and joined me. Then in the deep end of the pool as I was wading in the water, he brought my ring out of his bathing suit pocket. His hands were trembling.

"Cassie, I know I'm not always right, but I'll always do my best to be with you," he said. "Will you…"

And then the ring fell out of his trembling hand. It plummeted toward the bottom of the pool, and I was hoping it wouldn't get sucked into the drain. I kicked up my feet and dove to the bottom of the deep end. The ring whirled toward the drain. It spiraled as the drain pulled it in faster and faster. I snatched the ring just as it was reaching the pool floor drain.

When I popped out of the water and gasped for air Eric said, "You saved the day as always!" Then with his hands steadier he asked, "Cassie, will you marry me—and forgive me?"

I said, "yes," and knew that it was a yes to both questions. We embraced in the pool until the rooftop door swung open and Mr. Gillrot stepped out. "Am I late for the ceremony?" he said.

He was late for Mrs. Olive's ceremony, but right on time for the celebration of Eric's second proposal.

"What a crazy building we live in," he said. "I've paid my respects to Mrs. Olive, already. So, if I've missed the ceremony, that's okay. What a thoughtful, caring woman she was, and a great actress. And I bet you no one else in this crazy building even knew that."

He turned to walk away, and as the rooftop pool door slammed shut I thought maybe Mr. Gillrot had pinned down the perfect place to pick up the investigation. "Who else knew Dot Olive was a movie star? The famous Mallory Moore of *Rocky Lakes*?"

Eric looked at me and said, "Come to think of it, you figured out the connection between Dot and *Rocky Lakes*; we should assume other residents could have stumbled across that fact the same way."

"Mr. and Mrs. Rhodes had the *Rocky Lakes* DVD on their entertainment stand in their apartment, as well as a Barry Manilow CD. Copacabana was playing on the poolside CD player. Perhaps it was theirs? Do you think there's some connection between Mrs. Rhodes and Mrs. Olive?"

Eric splashed me with water. "I think if there is, you're the only person who could find it out." He embraced my arms and lifted me above the water, and kissed me. "I'm beginning to think only you can solve this case."

*****

The next day during my building rounds with Jet-Setter and Cashmere in tow, I slipped into the observatory. It was an old wooden building, with a white door that had a window. As I was walking by, I happened to glimpse Ben Harrison wasn't at the telescope. There was no harm in sleuthing while I got the chance. I opened the creaky door and the cats followed. I sat down in the old leather swivel seat and adjusted the telescope, which was pointing to the sky and turned it toward Parkstone Manor. Quickly, the apartments came into focus.

I could see Mrs. Kemper smoking on her balcony. This was a *no-smoking* building. She would have been using her hot pink cupcake lighter, but Eric had confiscated that as evidence. On the balcony below her, Mr. Gillrot was reading on a comfy wicker patio chair. Nothing suspicious there. Then off to the right and up a few flights there were Mr. and Mrs. Rhodes and Moola sitting on their balcony. Mrs. Rhodes' hair was perfectly styled in curls and she was wearing a lot of makeup. She must have an audition. I wondered if she knew Mrs. Olive through her acting connections. That could be it, although, Mrs. Rhodes was a lot younger and I don't know how their paths would have crossed.

Just then, I heard scuffling outside the door. The door flung open, and a large dark figure stood above me.

"Watcha doin?" he said.

It was Ben Harrison. I had to think quickly. "After you told me you see the moon most days, I decided to look in the sky and see for myself."

"It's in the other direction," he said, sitting down at the bench against the observatory's near wall. Then he stood up. "Let me see," he said, as I scooted off the chair. Then he peered through the telescope. "What have we got here? The telescope is pointed directly at the Rhodes' balcony. Were you spying?"

"The telescope must have moved," I said. "*I* was looking at the sky."

"Because right now it's focused on the Rhodes' balcony," he said.

I couldn't tell him I was doing some sleuthing during building rounds, and that I suspected Mrs. Rhodes of the crime, even though I didn't have any proof. Then I wondered if Ben ever spied on the neighbors and found out damaging information. That could be interesting.

And then as if he'd read my mind he said, "I try not to spy on the neighbors, but one time I did see Mrs. Olive out on her balcony, really dressed up fancy and her hair looked particularly nice. And there was Mrs. Rhodes on her balcony looking up at her angrily."

Hmm. There was definitely some link between the two women. I thought about the days before Mrs. Olive's death, and about the leak from the apartment above her—from the Rhodes' apartment. Every path seemed to lead back to Mrs. Rhodes.

I thanked Ben for his help and left the observatory to continue on rounds. Eric sent me a text message to make sure I wasn't spending my day worried about the case: "*Date night tomorrow night?*"

I wrote back: "*If the case is wrapped up.*" We had our eastern shore vacation planned for this weekend, too.

Chapter 12

The next morning I decided that if I was going to solve the crime of a starlet, I should look like one. I tousled my hair, applied a lot of lipstick, mascara, and eye shadow and wore a fancy black dress with a fun print—Scottie dogs with red bows. I almost didn't recognize myself. Then to top it off, I wore a tan, braided cloche hat.

There was a lot of activity going on, as Bethesda's annual dog show was underway right in front of Parkstone Manor. Many of the residents' dogs were participating in the show, and they had an early start on choosing seats.

The concierge desk was busy. Residents were picking up packages, checking to make sure the pool had re-opened, and were prepping their dogs for the runway sprint by walking them back and forth through the lobby.

"Go Moola!" Mrs. Rhodes said as the Chihuahua scurried through the lobby. Then she turned to me. "Cassie, are you going to the dog show?"

"I plan on stopping by," I said. "Is Moola ready?"

"This dog is so obedient and knows all of the commands," she said. "I think our Moola will bring home the top prize: a gold canine statue."

"I don't see why not," I said, watching the small dog sit and jump on command. She was even wearing a winner's outfit: a gold sparkling doggie shirt. It seemed like this pooch had the competition in a tough *paws*-ition.

"We can't wait to win," Mrs. Rhodes said. She was wearing a gold-colored knit shirt that matched Moola's, and a knee-length black skirt with bright flowers print.

As I stepped out onto the street in front of the Parkstone, I realized my fancy black dress with Scotties on it would be a huge hit at the dog show. The area was overflowing with people and most of the Parkstone residents were in attendance. The Berrys and the Rhodes were there. Mr. Eager had a front row seat and Ginnie Langford was at the foot of the stage. The two most notably absent were Jet-Setter and Cashmere, the Parkstone cats, who were more content curled up on the concierge desk.

I walked down the steps of the Parkstone's front hill and was greeted by some furry, lovable dogs along the way. Only one dog jumped up on me, and I was wondering if he thought the Scotties on my dress were real. There were large huskies and small Chihuahuas like Moola, who were making their way among the dozens of chairs lined up in rows in front of a large stage that included a podium and a runway. It was fun to get a sense of the show, but I probably wouldn't stay long. I waved to Parkstone residents Mrs, Kemper and Mrs. Canterbury. It was good to make an appearance.

I noticed cameras from local TV stations interviewing dog owners. Mrs. Rhodes was smiling in front of the nearest camera as she cradled Moola in her arms, and gestured wildly with the other. "We're just so honored to be taking part in Bethesda's Annual Dog Show," she said, "and I don't mean to brag, but our Moola here might just win the trophy and wag her tail all the way home."

The reporter looked startled by Mrs. Rhodes' surety and said, "That's quite a lot of confidence for such a small Chihuahua. Best of luck to you, Mrs. Rhodes. Jim, over to you."

I walked up to the chair where Mr. Rhodes was sitting, just as Mrs. Rhodes and Moola approached.

"Good luck to Moola," I said. "The entire Parkstone is rooting for her."

"Our fingers are crossed," Mrs. Rhodes said, "but our Moola doesn't need luck."

Mrs. Rhodes always had a comeback for everything. "Great, well, I just wanted to say a quick hello. I'll be going on my way."

I'd only walked a couple steps further when Moola darted in front of me. I gasped. She threw me off guard. and I screamed. She quickly ran circles around me, wrapping my legs in her leash, and causing me to lose my balance. My cloche hat went flying. Moola yelped as I fell right into Mr. Rhodes' lap.

"Moola!" Mrs. Rhodes reprimanded the dog, but the damage had already been done. I was mortified.

There I was wearing my beautiful black dress with the Scotties with red scarves print plopped down on Mr. Rhodes' lap. I stood up and untangled myself from Moola's leash. I think I'd seen enough of the dog show. I grabbed my cloche off the floor and said goodbye to the Rhodes. I walked back up the hill to the Parkstone to join Jet-Setter and Cashmere in the cool, air-conditioning inside. There were banging and hammering noises from the club room's renovations. I could stand the loud noises of the renovations more than I could stand the over-the-top dog competition.

Half an hour later, as I listened to the construction workers renovate the club room down the hallway, I was thinking maybe the dog show would have been less stressful. But then, I thought better of of that idea. I watched the competition from the front lobby window as Moola strutted across the runway. She obeyed every command from Mrs. Rhodes, who was smiling as she walked beside Moola. There was something about her smile that was menacing. And I believed that Moola, even though she was small, could cause a lot of destruction.

This wasn't the first time I had been disapproving of Moola. I thought back to the morning of the murder when I'd run into Mr. Rhodes and Moola in the rooftop pool vestibule. I remembered that I had been upset because Moola had shaken her wet fur all over my hot pink dress. Then a thought dawned on me. Mrs. Rhodes said then that they hadn't yet been to the pool; she had lied. Moola had obviously been *in* the pool. And the water she flung all over me had been the proof.

What if Mrs. Rhodes and Moola had been at the pool that morning? That changed everything. I had an idea. I placed the *"Will be back shortly,"* sign on the desk and headed up to the rooftop. Outside, it was extremely humid, as I walked poolside along the roof deck. The cabana, which had been fixed, was on my right. And everything now looked like it had before Mrs. Olive's murder.

I looked at some sparrows sitting in a row along the rooftop's cement wall. I tried to focus on what that morning could have been like for Mrs. Olive. The birds chirped. Mrs. Olive was afraid of birds. I remember her towel was slung over a chestnut tree branch in the far corner. What if she gotten out of the pool, and wanted to dry off? So, she began walking toward her towel…

Yes, that must have been it! Everything had been fine until a bird chased her, just like the pigeon had chased me out of the club house the other day. She must have run along the cement, but then, what if Mrs. Rhodes and Moola were in her way? If Mrs. Rhodes was sitting on a chaise, all she would have to have done is given Moola a command to 'go' and she'd have darted in front of Mrs. Olive and then jumped into the pool. And Mrs. Olive would've fallen head first into the cement, just like I'd fallen at the dog show. Now, the only question was why? What grudge did Mrs. Rhodes have against Mrs. Olive?

I couldn't think of any motive. My guess was, whatever the grudge was, it ended in Mrs. Olive being tripped by Moola and her leash.

I needed to get back to the concierge desk. The dog show would be wrapping up soon, and there would be an onslaught of busy residents who wanted dinner reservations, or guest rooms reserved, or an update on the parlor room renovations.

I quickly headed back downstairs, convinced I'd figured out the crime. At the concierge desk, I greeted residents coming home from the dog show. They were all smiles. Then I peered out the front window to see the Rhodes walking up the front lawn with the gold canine trophy and Moola at their side. The killer Chihuahua had won the dog show.

Mr. Rhodes looked proud, and Mrs. Rhodes' grin was as plastered on as the new parlor room wallpaper.

Once they stepped into the Parkstone, I congratulated them on their win, as Moola scampered across the lobby into the courtyard.

Then I decided now was the best time to nudge them into a confession.

In all the commotion, Mr. Rhodes stepped forward toward the concierge desk. "We'll need last minute reservations for two at Plum Orchard for tonight." He paused. "We're celebrating. And ask if they allow pets. Surely they'll make an exception for the winning Chihuahua."

I nodded. "I can call now and then come find you and Mrs. Rhodes in the courtyard," I said. "I wouldn't want to *trip* up your plans of spending time with Moola."

"Trip up?" he said. "No, it will be fine. Go ahead. We'll wait."

Mrs. Rhodes put the gold canine trophy on the concierge desk. "Thanks, Cassie."

"You bet," I said, picking up the phone and dialing the restaurant, which was on speed dial. I placed the reservations for 6 p.m. for a party of two. No pets allowed—even canine trophy winners—but something told me they could probably sneak Moola in in Mrs. Rhodes' purse. Then I decided to get bold and I asked, "I hate to think Mrs. Olive might still be alive today if it weren't for a certain canine."

Mrs. Rhodes gasped and said, "You're wicked!"

"I was re-enacting the events of the morning Mrs. Olive was murdered. And I believe Moola was running into the pool, just as Mrs. Olive was running away from a bird and toward her towel."

Mrs. Rhodes was fidgety and said, "That's simply not true. Moola and I weren't at the pool that morning. I told you. I was still searching for my missing swim cap, which Mrs. Olive stole!"

"But then you came back to the pool with Moola. I know Moola had already been to the pool because her fur was wet when I ran into her and Mr. Rhodes in the rooftop vestibule. I believe you had it in for Mrs. Olive, and you told Moola to run, so Mrs. Olive would trip over her leash and fall on the cement, hitting her head."

That's when Mr. Rhodes caved. He put both hands up in the air is if to surrender and said, "I was grilling. *They* were the ones at the pool."

The uncooked burgers in the trash must have been from Mr. Rhodes, who'd planned on barbequing, but then had a change of plans when Mrs. Olive died and he and Mrs. Rhodes needed to escape quickly. It was all making sense now.

Mrs. Rhodes put her hands on her hips. "I stand by my story that I was not at the pool the morning of the murder, and neither was Moola."

"So, it's your word against your husbands?" I said. "Why did you hate Mrs. Olive?"

Then in a fit of anger, she yelled and picked up the bouquet vase sitting on the side of the concierge desk. She lunged forward, hoisting the bouquet toward me. The metal vase was coming straight at me, and I ducked, holding the sides of my cloche hat. The vase crashed to the floor, and the water from the vase and the tulips spilled out. Then she ran to the courtyard. She was going to get the Chihuahua.

I called Eric and said, "I have the killer. It's Mrs. Rhodes and Moola. I'll need back up at the Parkstone."

"Cassie, wait for us…" I heard him say, but I was already hot on the trail.

Then I hung up the phone and Mr. Rhodes ran out the front door. I raced to the courtyard. Mrs. Rhodes, who now had Moola in her purse, was running across the courtyard toward the catwalk. When she approached the catwalk, she stopped to look back. We were staring at each other, and I was trying to anticipate her next move when she ran back toward me. "Cassie, you have no idea what you're talking about."

"Then why are you running?"

Just then, Moola jumped out of her purse and began running up the nearest crab apple tree. Mrs. Rhodes followed to get her. I stood in front of the tree. I had her cornered. Then she dropped Moola in her purse and took off up the tree. Where was she going?

I was afraid of heights. I couldn't chase her, but I needed to get over this fear if I wanted to catch the killer.

I dug my peep-toe shoe into the bark and used that leverage to hoist my body up to the next branch and the next. I didn't look down for fear I'd get dizzy and not want to continue. Mrs. Rhodes was already at the top branch glaring down at me.

Then, when I'd reached the middle of the tree she cackled and brought out her lighter.

"Don't burn the tree down," I said, but that just made her laugh even harder. She set fire to the branch I was holding onto, and the blaze tore through the branch super fast, just as she shimmied down the opposite side of the tree.

I had no choice but to jump. I was so afraid my arms were trembling. I was losing my grip.

Suddenly, I heard Eric's voice, "Cassie, jump! I'll catch you!"

Out of the corner of my eye, I saw Eric below. I didn't want to let go but the flames were tearing through the branch closer and closer. The heat was unbearable.

Chapter 13

I plummeted from the top of the tree and landed with a thud in Eric's arms. "I knew I could catch you," he said. "I'll never let you down."

I opened my eyes to notice there was a rip in my dress, where it had been torn on the branch. *Darn Moola and Mrs. Rhodes. What cruel actions!* "I'll never be jumping from that high up ever again," I said, staring up at the tree which was now ablaze. Then the firefighters bustled through the courtyard doors and began putting the fire out. I was hoping there wouldn't be too much damage. At least Royce had insurance on all the Parkstone's property.

Then a thought crossed my mind: *Where was Mrs. Rhodes and Moola?* I hugged Eric, and marveled at how good it felt to be on the ground. Now my fear of my tenth-floor balcony seemed conquerable.

Minutes later, the detectives found Mrs. Rhodes a few blocks away from the Parkstone attempting to escape on a RideOn bus, a public transportation bus that picks up passengers in communities around the Washington, D.C., metro area. When the detectives caught them Moola was whimpering, and Mrs. Rhodes looked a lot less confident in handcuffs. Her headband was askew after the chase and her red curls were in disarray. The only thing still perfect seemed to be Moola's gold sparkling t-shirt.

Later, as dog show employees took down the stage from the dog show, Eric and I stood on the front lawn of the Parkstone while detectives questioned Mrs. Rhodes.

Eric put his arm around me. "How'd you know it was Mrs. Rhodes?"

"It piqued my interest when they said Moola hadn't been to the pool that morning. I knew she'd been because she'd shaken her wet fur all over my dress. That Chihuahua had already dipped in the pool. Mr. Rhodes claimed he was at the grill behind the club house, so that left Mrs. Rhodes to watch Moola. But I still don't know why."

Mrs. Rhodes, who was now in the police car with the backseat door open, kicked at the floor, and Moola, who was still in her purse, howled. "I'll tell you why," she said. "You wicked concierge. I always wanted to be a movie actress, I didn't aspire to be in commercials. Cassie, guess who tried out for the role starring opposite Dot Olive in *Rocky Lakes*? Me. And I swear Dot had it in for me from the beginning. She was disinterested and put no effort into reading her lines correctly. I wouldn't be surprised if she even asked the casting director not to sign me. It's like it was my turn to show I was the best person for the role, and she was going to do everything to show otherwise."

I was glaring at the woman who'd just burnt down the branch I was clinging to earlier.

"And then you set fire to the set of *Rocky Lakes*, just like you set fire to the club room, and the crab apple tree" I said.

"Cassie, I wish you weren't such a good sleuth," she said. She petted Moola who was peeking out of the tote and said, "And that morning at the pool, my husband Dash just wanted to grill hamburgers and listen to Barry Manilow. Well, Dot wouldn't have it. She said after she got out of the pool and dried off that she was switching the music. She had to control everything. She may have controlled much of the *Rocky Lakes* set, but I wasn't going to let her have her way at the Parkstone, too."

"That's no excuse for murder," I said.

"How did I know she was going to die from the fall?" she said, as the police shut the door and drove away. Moola could be seen yapping in the rear window.

*****

After wrapping up the case, and after Eric and I took the Rhodes' dinner reservations for two at Plum Orchard, I promised Eric I'd be packed for our beach trip the next day. Then next morning, I put all the essentials—swimsuit, Parkstone towel, seersucker shorts, lightweight tops and brightly colored dresses—into my large Ted Baker suitcases in the trunk. Then I packed my Longchamp purse with sunglasses and a straw hat for a quicker trip up to Pinecone Bakery and the pool.

When I approached the catwalk I hesitated, and took a deep breath. *The catwalk wasn't that high up. At least not compared to the crabapple tree I'd fallen out of.* Without looking down, I balanced, as if I were a model on a runway and without looking to the sides, with cars whirring by on the street below, I sashayed across the catwalk. I was almost near the end when panic set in. What if I fell? My head was light. I felt dizzy. I grabbed the catwalk's wooden railing. Then I thought of falling from the crabapple tree. I could do this. Finally across the catwalk, I walked into the bakery to be greeted by cheers.

Mike, the pastry chef, looked up as he was whisking a bowl of cookie dough. "There's the sleuth! We knew you could solve it. Choose a dozen pastries, on us."

I forgot he had offered a sweet reward for finding Mrs. Olive's killer. Who was I to argue?

I selected a dozen variety cupcakes, vanilla, red velvet, chocolate, cookies and cream, and blueberry, which they boxed up speedily. All had decadent icing and cute fondant sayings like, "Summer Sweets" and "Baking's a Breeze." I was so caught up in the cupcakes that walking back across the catwalk didn't faze me. Not one bit.

When I arrived at the rooftop pool, Harold Eager was among a slew of residents there. He was lounging on a chaise near the cabana, which I ducked into and laid my Parkstone towel on a chaise, enjoying the shade. Hearing the shouts of glee from residents like Ginnie Langford and Ben Harrison in the pool made me wish Harold would give swimming a chance.

"Cupcake?" I said.

"Don't mind if I do," he said, taking a red velvet from the box.

"Doesn't this heat and humidity ever make you want to jump in?"

"I was very young when I followed my older brother into the pool, and didn't know how to swim. Luckily this was before a swim class I was supposed to be taking and there was a lifeguard on duty who jumped in and rescued me."

I sighed. "You should give swimming a second chance." And if any day was ideal for the pool, it was today with the 95 degree temperatures. The scorching heat was almost unbearable on the rooftop.

Good thing I was dressed comfortably, I thought, and it helped to be in the shade of the sturdy cabana. I put my sunglasses on, more for effect than anything, and noticed there was a swift breeze that made anything seem possible.

I took the other red velvet cupcake from the box and nudged Harold, who stepped cautiously to the shallow end and dipped in his feet.

The cabana's panels shifted slightly in the wind. Then Ginnie Langford appeared, wearing a dazzling sparkling red one-piece swimsuit and stepped into the cabana as she said, "Cassie, I know you're off duty right now, but I see pool-goers wearing their Parkstone swim caps, and I'm wondering why I didn't get one."

I folded the *Glamour* magazine I was reading and said not to worry. There were plenty left in a box behind the concierge desk. One more request, and then the eastern shore vacation started tomorrow.

THE END

ABOUT THE AUTHOR

Sherry Lodge has been writing for more than a decade for both print and online. She's written for local newspapers in both Massachusetts and Washington, D.C., where she currently writes and edits web material for a major non-profit organization.

In addition to writing, Sherry loves to watch golf, which inspired Kip Ace as one of the main characters in the first in her Cassie Hall mystery series—*Courtyard Corpse*. *Cabana Corpse* is the fourth in this series, following *Cloakroom Corpse* and *Club Room Corpse*. Sherry has a master's degree in journalism from Boston University.

www.ingramcontent.com/pod-product-compliance
Lightning Source LLC
Chambersburg PA
CBHW020343260626
47156CB00004B/1670